Night of the November Moon

Ann Carol Ulrich

Earth Star Publications

Night of the November Moon

Ann Carol Ulrich

Earth Star Publications
Cedaredge, Colorado

First Edition
Revised October 2016
Copyright © 1999 by Ann Carol Ulrich
All Rights Reserved

ISBN 978-0-944851-17-3

Cover art by the Author

Published in the United States of America

To the past, may it lie in peace.

To the future, may it continue.

To the now, which is all that really matters.

Chapters

Night of the November Moon

Ann Carol Ulrich

1

The Dream

"WINNIE!" HIS voice called in the distance.

"Rob!" Sobs choked me. I didn't know which way to turn. "Rob!" The wind carried my voice away. "Rob, I can't find you!" My breath rattled.

"Winnie, where are you?" Now his voice had grown fainter.

The wind whipped my skirt as I groped my way through branches and briars blocking my path. Darkness had overtaken day. My bare arms and cheeks stung from scratches.

"Winnie!" he continued to call further away.

The wind storm raged around me and I stumbled through the woods in agony. Where was Rob? Why didn't he hear me calling? I had to reach him.

Suddenly, through the trees I saw it. There it stood, silhouetted majestically against the lavender horizon, the huge old Victorian manor that towered above the sloping lawn. Thick shrubs and willows partially hid its three floors and four verandas. As I stepped from the woods, I gazed in awe. Why were there no lights?

Where was Rob?

Lightning flashes illuminated the manor as the wind continued to sweep over me. I started up the lawn. I knew someone must be inside.

I called for Rob, but my voice would not respond.

Then my legs grew wobbly and I felt immobilized. "Rob... I know you're there." The wind smothered my sobs. I slumped onto the moist, cold ground, exhausted.

The next thing I knew, Rob was holding me. I welcomed the security of his warm body and his voice whispered in my ear, "Don't cry, Winnie." It was the same soothing voice I remembered from long ago. "Didn't you hear me calling you?"

"Rob, I tried to find you. I came right away."

I was startled. The gentle brown eyes that I remembered suddenly appeared blue. And his hair, instead of reddish brown, was now blond.

"George... it's you!" I awoke then.

In my dream I had been at Pelton Manor. I had been with Rob Pelton, even been held in his arms. It was rare that I dreamed of Rob Pelton anymore. Ten years had passed since we last had seen each other. Yet every once in a while, he would weave his way into my most intimate dreams.

Only this time he had transformed into *George*. I turned my face into my pillow to cry, but like the dream, my tears were not real.

The room was cold. I pulled the covers over myself and heard the whistle of a train in the distance. The Grand Trunk crossed town not far from Pelton Manor, where I had just been in my dream. I strained to remember more. It was important to cling to each thread as it unraveled in the presence of my waking memory. I tried to go back to sleep. I wanted to keep dreaming. But already I could feel it loosening. The words Rob had soothed me with were now jargon phrases without meaning, and his face had turned into George's.

It was disturbing to think about Rob Pelton after all of these years, yet a part of me derived a small degree of pleasure in dredging up the past. I couldn't help it. I had been so young then.

Bits of the dream kept coming back to me during a hurried breakfast. I didn't want to be late for work. I hadn't had the job more than a couple of months, and if I didn't get there before the boss, the whole office would complain about the lousy coffee. Slipping into my coat, my eyes fell on the long-stemmed red roses in a glass on the sink. Now wilted, they reminded me of last night and George. The petals were brown because he had forgotten and left them in the car, where they had been exposed too long to the November night air.

Much to my relief, the car started right up. I climbed out to scrape the frost off the windows and saw someone hurrying toward me. I recognized my neighbor, JoAnn Gremel, bundled in a winter jacket and wool hat.

"Winnie, can you give me a lift?" JoAnn had short, dark hair and bangs. Her cheeks were rosy from the chill as she approached.

"It's my car again. I think it's the battery, or the carburetor, or... oh, who knows?" JoAnn pulled out a handkerchief and blotted the end of her nose.

"Get in." I finished the windshield, then climbed behind the wheel.

"You know what we need, Winnie?" JoAnn asked as I backed down the driveway.

"What?"

"Two good-looking hunks who can fix cars."

I hissed in protest. "I'm no mechanic, that's for sure, but I can do everything Alan used to... change the oil, put in anti-freeze, change a tire..."

JoAnn would be the last person to admit it, but she was one of those women who are helpless without a man. I figured JoAnn, now divorced, wouldn't stay single for long. I had known her many years. The two of us had been best friends in high school.

As I drove into the morning rush hour traffic through downtown Spundale, JoAnn prattled on about her car problems. My mind wandered back to my dream. We were heading nowhere near that part of town, yet I kept thinking about Pelton Manor and Rob. I remembered how beautiful the woods were surrounding Pelton Manor. One of Rob's and my favorite places to meet had been at the old abandoned mill in back of the Pelton property. Suddenly I longed to be there now.

"Winnie, aren't we going to work?" JoAnn's voice startled me back to reality. I sighed as I realized I had driven past the newspaper building. JoAnn laughed. "What were you thinking about? George?"

I swung into the other lane to turn the car around. "No, I was thinking about going out in the woods this weekend."

"*This* time of year?" scoffed JoAnn. "I always thought spring was the time of year for you bird nuts. Is George going with you?"

"Actually, I was thinking of going out by myself."

JoAnn sniffed. "Don't tell that to George."

I made no reply. JoAnn was responsible for introducing me to George Wyatt—one of her many matchmaking efforts. It was through the local Audubon Society chapter, of which I had been a member for several years. JoAnn had arranged for me to take George to one of the meetings, and somehow we had ended up going together to every meeting since.

Both JoAnn and I worked at the *Spundale Star,* our hometown weekly newspaper. We rode the elevator and parted on our floor. JoAnn worked in advertising sales. She had been with the paper for three years.

I unlocked the door to the front office, where I worked, and turned on the lights. My desk was behind a big counter. The two reporters' offices were down the hall and the production department was one big room in back. I heard a noise and was startled when Ralph Pendergast, the editor and publisher, stepped out of his office to greet me. He was an easy-going, eccentric man of about sixty.

"Good morning, Winifred."

"Oh, Mr. Pendergast, you're already here."

"Once in a while I like to be early." He grinned at me. "Better get those snow tires on soon."

"I know what you mean," I said.

He hovered over the coffee maker, as if trying to find the switch. I hurried over.

"I was just going to brew a pot," said Mr. Pendergast.

4

"Oh, I'll do it," I told him.

"Well... if you insist." He stepped aside.

I dumped out yesterday's old grounds. Once, when Mr. Pendergast had made coffee, he had used the grounds from the day before. I rinsed and filled the pot with fresh water at the sink. Assured that I had things under control, he sauntered back into his office. I liked Mr. Pendergast's congenial manner. He rarely got upset at anyone. I was comfortable working for him, and the job had done me wonders, helping me adjust to a new kind of independence.

Keith Campbell walked in a few minutes later. By now the coffee machine was making noises and Mr. Pendergast poked his head out of his room. "Come in here, Keith," he called to the reporter.

Keith turned to me and made a face. "Please, Winnie, tell me you made the coffee this morning."

I merely smiled and let Keith sweat awhile.

The morning passed swiftly. It was publication day, so the telephone rang a lot and things were buzzing in the back room. I didn't remember I was hungry until JoAnn came in just before one.

"Aren't you going to take some time off for lunch?"

I shut the file drawer. "What do you have in mind?"

"I thought we'd try that new place on South Hayward. The owners placed an ad this week. It sounds quite good."

I turned to Marion, the other woman working in the front office with me.

"Go ahead," said Marion.

"Sara Bronson called this morning," I told JoAnn as I pulled on my coat. "She's having some minor surgery. It looks like she won't be able to do her column next week."

"The gossip column?"

"No, she said she already turned that in. I mean the *Focus* column. You know, the one that features different people around town."

"Oh, that."

"Unfortunately, I haven't told Mr. P. yet."

"Why not?"

"He's been down in the press room since eleven-thirty."

When we arrived at the restaurant, we found it packed with people. I suggested we leave and find a place where we didn't have to wait, but JoAnn insisted on staying.

"Look, there's Shirley Peterson." She pointed across the dining room.

"Who?" I followed JoAnn as she weaved past waitresses and a group of customers on their way out.

"Shirley used to work at the *Star*," JoAnn called back over her shoulder. "You'll like her."

A light-haired woman in business attire had seen JoAnn and motioned toward her. "Why, JoAnn, how nice to see you."

JoAnn introduced us.

"Nice to meet you, Winnie. Won't you two join me? It's ridiculous to have to wait."

We sat down. I noted that Shirley was attractive and carried an air of sophistication. She smiled, revealing perfect teeth. "JoAnn, I haven't talked to you in ages. How's Jack?"

JoAnn's face tightened. She hadn't expected the question. But she tossed her head and shook it off with a laugh. "He's fine. Along with his new wife and baby."

Shirley's mouth fell open. Obviously she had not been aware of JoAnn's divorce. Shirley apologized, but JoAnn made light of it.

"Really, Shirley, getting rid of that scum was the best thing that ever happened to me."

A young waitress appeared at the table with a bus tray and towel. She did not appear to be too experienced as she nervously gathered up the dirty dishes and fumbled with some change.

"How's Mr. Pendergast?" Shirley's eyes focused on me. "How do you like working for him?"

"Oh, I like him."

Shirley sighed. "Dear old Ralph. There are times I wish I

still worked at the paper."

The waitress brought three menus. I ordered a pineapple and cottage cheese salad.

"Are you married, Winnie?" Shirley's gaze had fallen on my white gold solitaire wedding ring and diamond. I had not been able to get them off. I was so used to wearing them, I didn't think of the meaning.

"Well..."

"Hey, why are we discussing marriage?" interrupted JoAnn, always my defender when the subject came up.

"It's okay, Jo." I sipped my water.

"Oh, are you newly divorced?" Shirley continued to smile pleasantly.

"No, I'm a widow. Almost a year now."

JoAnn steered the conversation in another direction. "Shirley has three children. One of them is a carrier for the *Star*. What's his name again?"

"Greg," said Shirley, "and he's only had the route since school started a couple of months ago, but he's really stuck to it." Her cheeks sagged a little. "At least that's the way it used to be. Lately he's been... I don't know. I swear, he's ten years old and should know better than to believe everything he hears."

JoAnn shot me a puzzled look, then asked, "What's wrong? Is he bored with the job?"

Shirley sighed. "No, I don't think it's that. Greg is serious when it comes to earning money. But he seems to have developed a kind of paranoia the last couple of weeks when he has to deliver the paper. He's fine until Thursday comes around."

"So am I," I quipped.

Shirley looked around. "I wonder where our food is. Anyway, I found out just this morning what Greg's problem is."

The waitress appeared with napkins, silverware and drinks.

When she left, Shirley continued, "He will *not* go near the old manor on Pelton Drive, unless someone goes with him. He's afraid of ghosts. Can you imagine?"

I was startled by the mention of Pelton Manor. I was suddenly reminded of my dream. JoAnn seemed reminded of something, too. I could feel the sudden stir in her.

Shirley went on. "Well, after all, a ten-year-old boy is very impressionable. Halloween was just a couple of weeks ago, and some of his friends must have planted the idea in his head. You know how kids are. And with such an old house in the area, especially one as spooky-looking as the Pelton estate..."

"It's a beautiful home," I interrupted. I opened my napkin over my lap. "Much too nice for ghosts."

"Oh, then you're familiar with the place?"

"It's been many years," I replied. I couldn't help feeling that same warmth and excitement that had swept over me upon waking that morning. I recalled the sound of the train in the distance that had brought me out of my dream state. The railroad tracks ran not too far from Pelton Manor, and as a high school girl I had lain awake nights, listening to the distant train whistles and rumbling of freight cars, thinking about Rob.

"Then you already know about the family tragedy last spring."

I stared at Shirley. "What tragedy?" I felt my heart begin to race.

"Oh, you must have. It was in the papers." Shirley's eyes grew wide. "One of the Pelton sons died in that house."

For an instant I seemed to lose all sense of time. Then I felt JoAnn touch my arm. "Winnie, you're pale. Are you feeling all right?"

"Which one of the Pelton sons?" I heard myself whisper. But I already knew it couldn't be Rob, for I would have heard about it if anything had happened to Rob.

"The oldest. I can't remember his name."

"Benjamin."

"Yes," said Shirley.

My throat felt dry. "Benjamin's dead?"

"You didn't hear about it because you were in Hawaii last spring with your parents," JoAnn explained. "I remember reading about it."

"What happened?" I demanded.

"He was found dead at the bottom of the staircase," Shirley recalled. "It was said to be an accident, but a good friend of my mother works for the Peltons. Apparently *she* doesn't believe it was an accident."

I hung my head. "Oh my God..."

JoAnn said nothing. I wondered why on earth JoAnn had kept this information from me.

"Then, shortly after, his father died in a rest home," continued Shirley. "Mr. Pelton suffered a stroke right after it happened, so it was really a double tragedy for the family."

The food arrived, but my appetite had been destroyed. I tried to eat what I could of my salad, but memories kept flashing through my head. How could Rob's older brother and their father, Otto Pelton, be dead?

What bothered me most was how it had been kept from me for so long. Why hadn't anyone told me?

2

The Assignment

"YOU'VE BEEN awful quiet since lunch." JoAnn sat in the front office after it closed. I was putting the last of my work away.

"I have?"

"You didn't say a word after we left the restaurant. If it was Shirley... well, I know she can carry on once she gets going, but she doesn't mean any harm."

"Don't be silly, Jo. Shirley's very nice." I really wanted to tell JoAnn how upset I was with *her* for never telling me about the Peltons. How could she have withheld information like that from her best friend, particularly when she knew how involved I had once been with Rob?

"Winifred," called Mr. Pendergast.

I turned and saw the boss standing outside his office. "Yes, Mr. Pendergast?"

"I need a word with you."

"It won't take long," I assured JoAnn. I followed Mr. Pendergast into his office.

"Winifred, I've been giving some thought about Sara," he began.

I slapped my cheek. "Oh no! I forgot."

Mr. Pendergast leaned forward. "Excuse me?"

"Oh, Mr. P., I meant to tell you about her. She called this morning while you were down in the press room. I was going to tell you after lunch. I've just... had other things on my mind."

Mr. Pendergast settled back in his chair. "Marion gave me the message. Actually, I wanted to bounce an idea off you. What do you think about filling in for Sara while she's gone?"

Perplexed, I didn't know what to say. "I'm not sure I understand."

"Would you be interested in taking over Sara's column while she's gone?" Mr. Pendergast sat up straight and folded his hands on his desk.

"You're asking *me* to take over Sara's column?" I asked.

"It shouldn't interfere with your normal duties, I don't think. If it does, let Marion or one of the other girls in back help you out a little."

I felt flattered that he had asked me to write in Sara's place, but wondered why he had chosen me. "But, Mr. Pendergast, I really don't know anything about reporting."

"Oh, nonsense," he growled. "Reporting is nothing. Besides, the kind of writing you'll be doing will be fun. It will be like your little nature column, only more diverse."

How could I explain to him that writing my weekly two-inch column on birds and wildlife was hardly even a chore as far as I was concerned? Taking over Sara's column would involve talking to people, researching in depth, writing *professionally*.

"Why are you asking me, Mr. P.?"

"Because I think you have a lot of appeal, Winifred. People are comfortable around you and I believe you'll do the best job."

My hands were sweating. "I'm sure a lot of other people on the staff could do better. What about Keith or Laura?"

"The reporters are working overtime as it is," said Mr. Pendergast. "Besides, Winifred, I've chosen you for the assignment. If all goes well, Sara will be back in a couple of weeks. Do you accept?"

I smiled helplessly. He was one man it was hard to turn down. Finally I sighed and asked, "Just what do you want me to do?"

When we walked down to the parking lot, JoAnn asked me

what that had been all about.

"I think I have to write an article," I replied.

"So? Don't you write one every week?"

"That's different. He wants me to write a *real* story, Jo. Now I'm not sure I can do it. Oh, why did I let him talk me into it?"

"What do you get to write about?"

"I don't know yet. A human interest story, like what Sara's been doing."

The wind blew and JoAnn pushed her dark hair aside. "Well, you could do a piece on the high school. You've got George to help you out."

But I didn't want to write about the high school. There was enough in the paper about the local schools, especially on the sports page. "I should be able to find something more challenging than that," I commented.

We rode in silence for a while, and then JoAnn spoke up. "Winnie?"

"What?"

"I know what's been on your mind. It's no wonder you've been quiet."

I said nothing. The car cruised into the residential area of Spundale.

"You've been thinking about Rob Pelton, haven't you?"

JoAnn did at times seem able to read my mind. I remembered in high school, it had been impossible to keep a secret from her. "Come on, I know you have," she prodded. "I saw how you looked at lunch when Shirley talked about the old manor."

I suddenly felt like getting it all out in the open. "Jo, why didn't you tell me about the Pelton deaths?" I blurted. "Why did you keep that from me?"

JoAnn dug her lipstick out of her purse and dabbed some on.

"Well, Winnie, I'm sorry, but you were on vacation at that time. Was I supposed to remember everything I read?" She sighed. "You were gone for two whole months."

12

I tried to concentrate on the road. "You had to know I would be interested."

"Honestly, I forgot all about it."

I looked at her in a flash of anger, but JoAnn's pleading face convinced me that perhaps my resentment was unfounded. Maybe she actually had thought nothing of it. After all, she never knew the Peltons. On the other hand, it bothered me to have lived these past months not knowing.

"I wonder if Rob ever married," said JoAnn after a long silence.

I didn't say anything right away. Then, as I turned the car down JoAnn's street, an inspiration hit me. "Jo, you know what I think I'll do?"

"What?"

"Write a piece about Pelton Manor."

"Huh?"

"Why not? It's one of the oldest estates in Spundale. I'll bet there's a lot of historical information about that place."

"Sounds like a possibility," said JoAnn, then gave me a dubious look. "Are you sure you want to go there? I mean, after all, Winnie, it might dredge up a lot of emotions."

I stared straight ahead as I drove, then glanced at her and said, "I don't see how it could hurt ... after all these years."

I decided to call the Peltons tomorrow and find out if they would be interested in giving me an interview. "Anybody would be happy to be featured in the *Star,* don't you think?" I commented.

"Uh-*huh.*" JoAnn had a knowing look on her face.

"Now what?"

"Maybe you'll get the inside scoop on Rob."

I was quick to reply. "JoAnn, that was ten years ago." I dropped JoAnn off at her house, then drove the few short blocks home. I noticed how it was getting darker earlier each night now that it was November. Dusk was already settling in as I parked the Dodge in the driveway. I lingered a few moments before getting out.

As I caught a glimpse of my face in the rear-view mirror I began to think. *Ten years*—had it really been that long ago?

Rob Pelton had entered my life during my second year of high school. He had been a senior, two years older than I, and oblivious to the fact that I even existed. I had idolized him the entire school year. JoAnn had never understood what it was I thought was so fascinating about Rob, who was quiet and studious. She claimed he was attractive enough, but dull. JoAnn used to tease me that it was his family's wealth that I was interested in. It hadn't been that at all.

Once, in the hall between classes, I had accidentally bumped into him and he had smiled at me. But the rest of the year he appeared not to notice me at all. Later, I found out he was just as shy as I was. When he graduated, I thought my heart would break. I was sure I would never see him again.

Then the miracle happened. Rob had come to the first summer teen dance with a group of his friends. To my astonishment, he sought me out of the crowd and asked me to dance. I had then found out my feelings for him had not been in vain. We continued to date throughout the summer. Our innocent young love blossomed and grew in ways I had only dreamed.

Before Rob left for college in the East that fall, he had tried to explain to me how important it was to him to receive a full education. He hoped to become a doctor. But at the time, I had been too blind and too selfish to understand. Having a boyfriend was new to me. I didn't want to lose him. He promised to write and to see me during college breaks, but I was never to see him after that summer.

Although I wrote to him several times, I only received one letter back. Doomed to a lonely junior year at Spundale High, I resented the fact that Rob never called me or came home on weekends. Of course it was a long ways to travel, but even during Christmas and Easter I heard nothing from him.

I couldn't bear the thought of Rob having found another girl, so I continued to wait patiently and miserably. When summer came and Rob didn't come home, I began to feel differently. JoAnn was having dates and was encouraging me to have fun, too.

At first I was reluctant, but when my senior year began, I gave in and let a few boys take me out. Among these had been Alan Grant, a track athlete who made me the envy of the other girls. It wasn't long before Alan and I had a steady relationship. By the time graduation rolled around, I realized I really loved Alan. His companionship had helped absorb some of the hurt I still felt over Rob Pelton.

It was getting cold sitting in the car. I got out and checked the mailbox. There was a postcard from Arizona, where my parents presently resided. I took it inside and read it. There was one piece of interesting news: "*We are planning on driving up to Michigan for Thanksgiving. Will let you know more about this later.*"

Before I could reflect on this, the telephone rang. I answered it and a warm, masculine voice met my ears. "Hi, Fred."

"Oh hello, George." I suddenly remembered he was coming over that evening. "What time should I expect you?"

"That's what I'm calling about," he said. "I have all these exams to correct tonight, and I thought I was going to get some help, but Meyers is in bed with the flu. It'll take me all night to get them done."

"Well, can't I help you correct them?"

"How much chemistry did *you* have in college?" he asked.

I laughed. "Never mind."

"But I'll make it up to you tomorrow night, I promise. We'll go out for dinner and maybe a little dancing."

I pondered this a moment. "Hm, sounds like fun." I told George not to work too hard and hung up. Ever since the Audubon meeting in September, we had been going out on a casual basis. I insisted there wasn't anything serious between George and myself, although JoAnn and everyone else liked to think there was. I simply enjoyed George's company. He was a chemistry teacher at the high school. He had a certain personality that made me feel at ease. I was perfectly content just to remain his companion.

After a light supper, I dug out the old high school annuals and went through them. There was still a lot on my mind from the day's events. I paged through track shots of Alan, which he had autographed, but mostly made a fool out of myself by finding pictures of Rob Pelton and remembering how I used to pine over him.

It turned out to be a lonelier evening than if I had switched on the TV or settled down with a good book. An emptiness I had not felt in months began to eat at me.

3

Turned Away

I STILL remembered, even after all these years. I didn't need to look in the telephone directory. Rob's old telephone number was fresh in my mind as I punched the seven digits on my office phone the next morning.

"Hello." It was a woman's voice that answered.

I recognized Rob's mother. "Mrs. Pelton?"

"Yes, this is Mrs. Pelton. Who is this?"

In my official newspaper voice, I introduced myself and explained about the article I wanted to write. I prayed Mrs. Pelton didn't notice the tremor in my vocal cords. "And I was wondering if you would let me have an interview."

There was a pause. "Well, I don't know..." My heart hammered. I couldn't let her say no. Suddenly I was at a loss for words. Then Mrs. Pelton added quickly, "All right, I'll talk to you."

I sighed in relief. We arranged for a meeting at the manor that afternoon, then I thanked Mrs. Pelton.

"Uh... what did you say your name was again?"

"Winnie Grant." When I hung up, I felt relieved, but a trifle frightened by the whole thing. I wondered if Mrs. Pelton would remember me.

Mr. Pendergast came out of his office just then and asked, "Winifred what are you so puzzled about?"

I told him about my appointment with Mrs. Pelton.

"Good girl."

"But, Mr. P., I'm a little nervous. I hope I'll know what questions to ask her."

Mr. Pendergast beckoned me into his office, where I received a brief lesson in journalism.

I WAS hardly aware it was Friday afternoon with the weekend ahead. I drove my car across the railroad tracks on the edge of town. This was a quiet, prosperous section of Spundale, where a lot of the older homes had been built. Among these was Pelton Manor.

Memories from the past filled my mind as I turned onto Pelton Drive. There had been a particular November day ten years ago, when JoAnn and I had walked past the manor. How hopeful I had been, trying not to appear conspicuous, but looking to see if it would be a Saturday that Rob had decided to come home.

As I neared the manor, I felt the old tingle in me, just like in my dream yesterday morning. I chided myself, scornful because of the old feelings. After all, things had changed after ten years. I was no longer that pitiful sixteen-year-old suffering from unrequited love. I turned into the long, winding driveway that led up to the manor and parked under a tree.

For a long moment I sat and studied the old house before I got out of the car. The three-story Victorian home with its vine-covered roof overlooked the sloping lawn. Carefully manicured shrubbery surrounded the front porch. Bare-branched, gigantic willow trees towered over the house. Their crooked limbs gave the place the eerie quality of a Halloween spectacle.

Finally, I got out of the car and walked up the stairs of the vine-covered porch, my purse and note pad with me, and rang the doorbell. After a minute, one of the doors opened and a stocky, gray-haired woman, wearing an apron, met me.

"Is Mrs. Pelton in?"

"Who may I say is calling?" Apparently the woman was some kind of servant, perhaps the housekeeper.

"I'm Mrs. Grant from the *Spundale Star*. Mrs. Pelton is expecting me."

The woman stepped back to let me enter. I found myself inside the larger than normal foyer. Facing me was the staircase, carpeted in velvety red. The housekeeper, or whomever she was, disappeared into one of the hallways. I was immediately captivated by the elegance of the antique furniture, the vividness of some old paintings on the walls. There was that dusty, dry, undefined smell—perhaps of old wood—which I often associated with old houses.

Footsteps approached. I turned to greet a young and attractive woman who was tall and blonde with heavily made up blue eyes and high cheek bones. The casual slenderness of her walk reminded me of a cat. She wore a dressy light blue pantsuit, white sandals and a flashy gold necklace.

"I am Mrs. Pelton," she announced without smiling, as if I were a solicitor.

"*You're* Mrs. Pelton?" I was baffled.

"That's right." The ends of her lips curled up in a cat-like half-smile.

"I'm Winnie Grant from the *Spundale Star*. I had an appointment at two o'clock..."

"Oh, you must have come to see *Irene*."

"Yes." I knew that Rob's mother's name was Irene.

"Well, she's not here now."

"But I'm a few minutes early." I glanced at my watch. "Perhaps if I wait..."

"I'm afraid my mother-in-law has gone out for the afternoon. I'll tell her you came by." She moved toward me, sort of forcing me out the door. "Mrs. Grant, is it?"

"Yes. That's funny. She told me on the phone..."

"I'm sure whatever Irene told you she got all mixed up. I'll tell her you came, Mrs. Grant."

I was outside now and the door shut on me. I returned to my car, flustered. This had not been at all what I had expected. Mrs. Pelton's reference to two o'clock had sounded most definite over the telephone. I glanced back at the porch. Who was the blonde woman who also called herself Mrs. Pelton?

Starting up the engine, I suddenly noticed something peculiar in one of the high, third-story windows of the manor. Something had moved out of place. It was as if someone who had been there a moment ago had darted quickly out of sight. My eye had caught only the movement. Or had it been just my imagination?

The more I thought about it while I drove away, the less likely it seemed, and I soon put it out of my mind.

4

More Questions

"BACK SO soon?" Mr. Pendergast found me daydreaming at my desk.

"I got stood up," I confessed.

"Well, that happens." He started toward his office, then stopped and turned around. "Just in case you become discouraged, I made a list of alternative ideas. Perhaps one of them will interest you."

"Oh, I haven't given up yet."

"That's the spirit, Winifred."

I spent the rest of the afternoon proofreading legal notices and helping Marion with the billing. Fridays were generally slow in the office. My mind kept returning to Pelton Manor. After I finished the necessary work, I wandered over to the file cabinets and pulled out some papers from the morgue. All of the old issues of the newspaper were kept on file in the morgue. I wanted to look up the story the *Star* had run on the tragic death of Benjamin Pelton. I didn't know the date, but JoAnn had mentioned it had happened during my trip last spring.

I browsed for half an hour before I finally found what I was looking for. The story had made the front page of Section B. It didn't compare to the tale Shirley Peterson had given at lunch the day before. It told only that Benjamin's death had been ruled accidental by the coroner's office and that he had been pronounced dead on arrival at the hospital. There was no mention of his father's stroke, but then I hadn't expected to read about that in the article.

I returned the morgue to its drawer, then eagerly began to search the obituary records for the obits on Benjamin and his father. Without too much trouble I found them. Benjamin's didn't tell me anything I didn't already know except that he had left a widow, Marcia. That must have been the young blonde woman I had talked to over at the manor, I decided.

Because Otto Pelton had been such a prominent citizen of Spundale, his obituary was longer. I read through it.

> Otto Pelton, 65, life-long resident, died Friday at Spider Lake Convalescent Home outside of Fremont. He was born in Spundale and was former president of Pelton Enterprises, and served on the Spundale School Board for many years.

I skipped over a lot of his accomplishments, then read:

> He was preceded in death by a son, Benjamin. Surviving are his wife, Irene; a son, Robert; a daughter, Rose; two aunts: Pearl and Ophelia Pelton; and several nieces and nephews.
>
> Graveside services will be held at 2 p.m. Monday in Spundale Memorial Gardens. Friends may call from 7 to 9 Sunday evening at the Pelton home, 1645 Pelton Drive.

A couple of things I found interesting about the article. Otto Pelton had died at Spider Lake Convalescent Home, a rest colony located several hours' drive northwest of Spundale. I had heard of the place. Spider Lake was an upscale private resort for convalescing senior citizens. I also found it odd that friends of the deceased were invited to call at the manor instead of at a funeral parlor.

After work I told JoAnn how I had failed to get my story on the Peltons.

"I'll bet it brought back plenty of memories by going there," said JoAnn.

"It did."

"Well, you know what they say. You can't go back. You can't relive the past."

It bothered me to think about what JoAnn had said. I knew I could never be sixteen again, but I still felt those same longings at times. All the hurt had not buried the tenderness I still felt toward Rob Pelton. If anything, the reason behind that hurt was probably why I kept thinking about him. I had to know why, why he had stopped writing, *why* he had quit caring. It seemed I could never rest until I knew.

5

Night on the Town

THE DOORBELL rang and I panicked. I struggled into my clothes and fumbled for the zipper. Running the brush one last time through my hair, I hurried into the living room.

George Wyatt stood patiently outside. I opened the door and let him in. He was dressed up tonight in a light blue turtleneck sweater and suede jacket. His rich blue eyes met mine with an eager smile. His hair was blond and plentiful with darker brows. He looked superb in his attire, not at all like any high school chemistry teacher I had known.

"I'm almost ready, George."

He strolled into the room, a coat over his arm. "It's getting cold out," he said. "Better wear a warm jacket, Fred."

I opened my closet in search of one. George had picked up on my childhood nickname, Fred, short for Winifred. "Where are we going tonight, George?"

"It's a surprise."

En route to the restaurant, we chatted and I told George I had to write an article.

"No kidding. In addition to your column?"

"That's right. It's only for a couple of weeks, though."

"Well, what's it going to be about?"

"The Pelton family."

"Who? I never heard of them."

"Probably because you've only lived in Spundale a year,"

24

I commented. I didn't want to explain to him how I had once dated a member of the Pelton family.

We had dinner at a lavish restaurant north of the city. George had made reservations and the food was delicious. It took my mind off a lot of things, especially work. George kept me entertained by his witty adventures in the classroom and I felt so free and comfortable with him. I found myself laughing and giggling louder than usual, but it wasn't until I got up from the table that it hit me. I hadn't realized that I had been drinking Burgundy wine in successive glassfuls since we had arrived. When George had ordered the bottle, I thought for sure he was crazy. We wouldn't get through half that bottle. But now it was almost empty.

I made an excuse to slip away to the ladies' room and started out alone. My head felt light and the suspended chandeliers appeared to wobble with each step. I thought how ridiculous I must have sounded, laughing my fool head off.

"Are you all right, Fred?" I felt George grasp my arm.

I exploded into giggles. I couldn't help myself. Then I sighed, very much upset with myself. "Oh George, why did you let me drink all that wine?"

"I was too busy talking to notice, I guess. Here, let me walk you over."

"No, I'll be all right," I protested. "People must think I'm a real lush. I can make it." I started off in the direction of the restrooms and almost bumped into a waitress carrying a tray of food.

When I came out of the ladies' room, George had my coat. "I already paid the check. Ready to go dancing?"

"Dancing? In *my* condition?"

George led me toward the door. Without warning, I slipped and lost my balance. Luckily, George caught me before I fell. "Fred!" He laughed. "You've got to be more careful."

My face burned with embarrassment. It seemed to me that everyone in the dining room was staring at this curly-haired female drunk who tripped over her own feet. "Take me home,"

I moaned.

"No such thing. The night is young." George's face was so bright and hopeful, I couldn't help but follow as he led me to the car. "A little exercise ought to revive you," he said and started up the engine.

I closed my eyes and let my head fall back against the seat. I had developed a slight headache. The soft bounce of the pavement was relaxing me. George turned his radio on and I actually did doze off for a few minutes.

The next thing I knew, we had arrived at the town's most frequented bar. JoAnn was always telling me about the times she went there. I was a little provoked at the loud music at first, mostly due to my headache. But George surprised me by getting right up and dancing. Before long I came out of my stupor and had a great time. I couldn't remember how long it had been since I had had so much fun. It had certainly been more than a year.

At midnight we left, pleasantly exhausted, and stopped at an all-night coffee bar. It was starting to get crowded as we walked in, but we were lucky enough to find a small table.

"Have a good time?" George looked across at me with his warm smile.

"Yes, George, it was really fun." I suppressed a yawn.

George reached across the table, took my hand in his, and clasped it. It felt warm and comforting. "So did I."

I didn't know why it should have occurred just at that moment, but suddenly I thought of Rob Pelton and I could not get the memory of his face out of my mind. As I sat across the table from George, I stared into an image of Rob Pelton's face. I remembered how, in my dream, Rob's face had turned into George's. A second later it faded.

"What's wrong?" George looked concerned.

"Nothing." I sipped my coffee.

For a long moment George was silent. Then he asked, "Winnie, have you ever thought you might want to get married again?"

Married? Where had *that* come from, I wondered. I blinked and tried to focus. "Oh, well... I don't know. I suppose... maybe some day."

There was a pause as we both took long sips from our cups. I avoided his stare and waited nervously to see if he would say anything more.

Finally, George sighed and put his coffee down on the table. For the first time I noticed he was behaving in a peculiar fashion, as though he had something definite on his mind. But I knew George better than for him to be contemplating marriage, of all things.

"Why do you ask?" I asked in a tired voice.

He immediately cheered up. "No reason really. I'd just like to get you talking. You do too little of that, you know."

The waitress came around and refilled our cups.

"Sometimes it helps to open up," prompted George. "You've never told me much about your life, or about your late husband."

I knew what he was trying to do. I didn't know how much he had learned from JoAnn, but I just wasn't in the mood for delving into that past right now. "I'd rather not talk about it."

We were silent for a long minute. Again I waited for him to say more. George didn't push. "Hey, I had a great time tonight."

I looked up into his smiling face with the boyish blue eyes that seemed to twinkle at me from time to time. An unexpected wave of desire flooded through me in that moment and I quickly looked down into my cup. "I had a great time, too, George." My heart was pounding and I envisioned what it might be like if he were to kiss me. Thank goodness he never had. I didn't have to worry about George taking advantage of me, that was for sure.

"I'll take you home," George said, interrupting my thoughts.

We drank up what was left in our cups, then left.

6

The Interview

SLEEPING LATE on the weekends had become a habit with no one to disturb me. Saturday was half gone before I remembered there was an article to write that was due Monday. I considered myself lucky to have only a slight headache as a reminder of the night before.

Shortly after one o'clock I gathered my note pad and pen and drove toward the edge of town to call on the Peltons. This time my hopes were not as high. I wondered if I would be turned away again.

The day was mild. The sun peeked out from the clouds only moments at a time. As I turned my car onto Pelton Drive, I felt a flutter from within. Would I learn anything about Rob, I wondered. Would they tell me where he was living now, and if he had gotten married?

"Keep your mind on business," I chided myself as I passed tall trees near the cemetery. I pulled into the winding driveway and parked. Starlings called from high branches as I gathered my courage and stepped out of the car. The acrid smell of dead leaves filled the air. The wind stirred little piles of them as I made my way up to the porch. I couldn't help feeling a little panicky as I rang the doorbell and waited.

The door opened and this time Rob's mother stood before me. I noticed how much thinner and grayer the woman looked since I had last seen her. "Hello, Mrs. Pelton. My name is

Winnie Grant. I'm with the *Spundale Star*."

Mrs. Pelton nodded. "Please come in."

I stepped into the foyer. "Is this a good time to interview you for the article? I know I probably should have telephoned first."

Mrs. Pelton studied me. "Weren't you supposed to come yesterday?"

I was about to explain how I had come by the day before, but the young blonde woman who had met me yesterday came down the staircase. I smiled at her. "Hello again."

The younger woman forced a smile.

"Come into the living room, won't you please?" Mrs. Pelton led me into a large room, carpeted in white, with tasteful antique furniture and plush drapes at the huge Victorian windows. She beckoned me to sit down at an exquisite Queen Anne sofa, then took a seat across from me. She turned to the blonde woman who had followed us in.

"This is my daughter-in-law, Marcia," she explained. I had already guessed that the young woman must be Benjamin's widow. Marcia took a seat next to her mother-in-law.

"Would you care for some coffee or tea?" Mrs. Pelton offered.

"No, thank you." I didn't want to impose.

"Well, *I'd* like some. Marcia, has Mrs. McCloskey left for town yet?"

"I'll go check on her." Marcia hastened off. Her movements appeared very cat-like as they had yesterday.

I studied Mrs. Pelton for a moment. She had changed since ten years ago. She wore her silver hair neatly styled on top of her head. Her face seemed creased with age, and she had lost some weight. I tried to envision the cheerful, more robust woman I had known as Rob's mother.

"So what questions did you wish to ask?" prompted Mrs. Pelton.

I tried to clear my mind of the haunting memories. "Well, what I'm... you see, I thought..." I could have kicked myself for my lack of poise. Finally, I sighed and said, "If you could give me some historical background on the Pelton family... I understand this house also has quite a history."

If Mrs. Pelton noticed my nervousness, she didn't acknowledge it. I was glad Marcia had left the room. "Yes," she said, "the house was built by my husband's grandfather in 1881."

"Was he the original Pelton who settled here and helped start the town?"

"Yes, James Pelton and his wife Amelia moved here from Boston. Would you care to see some old photographs?"

When I eagerly nodded, Mrs. Pelton walked over to an old, beautifully refinished rolltop desk, and removed a large, dusty picture album. "Perhaps this will be of some help." She blew on it, which created a small cloud of dust, then brought it over and laid the book on the coffee table.

"This is wonderful." I scribbled notes as fast as I could while Mrs. Pelton began to tell how the original homestead had been just the front half of the manor. The addition, as well as the third floor, had been built by James' son, Christopher Pelton, after James' death.

"Was this son, Christopher, your husband's father?" I paged through the huge album carefully. There were some old, yellowed photographs of Pelton Manor as it had first stood.

"Yes, he was," said Mrs. Pelton. "Christopher had two sisters, Pearl and Ophelia. They live just down the lane in back of the manor."

"They're still living?"

Mrs. Pelton nodded. "Oh yes. A couple of kooks, those two sisters. They never married. That makes them spinsters, am I right?"

I smiled politely, then felt a sneeze coming on. Dust from the album had gotten up my nose. Marcia entered, carrying a tea pot. Behind her was the stocky, gray-haired lady who had answered the door yesterday. She set a tray of cups with sugar and cream on the coffee table, and eyed me curiously before she left.

I sneezed into my fist, then closed the album. Irene Pelton

continued as she poured our cups. "Of course, Christopher Pelton is now dead, and so is his wife, Katherine. They had two children, Otto and Anna, who is now dead."

I looked up from scribbling to catch a puzzled expression flash across Marcia's face. Mrs. Pelton noticed it and suddenly recalled something. "Of course, I mean to say they are both dead."

Before I could question her further, Mrs. Pelton began talking rapidly. "You see, my husband Otto suffered a stroke last spring. It was a terrible, terrible time for us when my eldest son..." The word caught in her throat.

Marcia stepped forward. "Benjamin was my husband. He died in an accident last spring."

"You won't print any of this, will you?" implored Mrs. Pelton.

"Of course not," I assured her.

She went on, "You see, when my husband discovered our son, he had the stroke right then and there, and we had to rush him off to the hospital." Her voice choked. "He died a few weeks later."

Marcia handed her mother-in-law a napkin, and Mrs. Pelton wiped a tear from her eye and sniffled. I felt uncomfortable, almost like I was intruding. Although I was curious to know more, to find out exactly what the details of Benjamin's death had been, I hadn't come to pry into their private lives. I sat and waited patiently for Mrs. Pelton to recover from her grief spell, then proceeded with the interview.

James Pelton, I discovered, had been active in organizing the town of Spundale, and his son Christopher had been an editor for the first local newspaper. His daughter, Anna, had been a schoolteacher. The Peltons had prospered through business and real estate in the ensuing years.

For some reason I was mostly interested in the manor itself. I hoped they would ask me to tour it, but they didn't. And I didn't feel right about asking to be shown through the manor.

Every minute I was there, Rob was on my mind. I couldn't

shut him out. He had grown up in this house, like his father and his grandfather before him. This was Rob's home. But I was sure Mrs. Pelton didn't recognize me, though I had hoped she would. I wanted to ask about Rob, and find out what he was doing with his life. I was on the verge of confessing to them that I had dated Rob in high school, then quickly decided against it.

As the minutes ticked away on the tall grandfather clock in the corner, I realized it was getting late. My note pad was full of information for my article and I had already taken up too much of their time.

"Is there anything else we can tell you?" Mrs. Pelton asked patiently for the second time.

"No." I sighed, then packed my pen and pad into my purse and stood up to leave.

A door closed from the next room. Footsteps ran up the staircase to the second floor. I heard a female voice singing. It gradually faded.

"Thank you for the tea," I said with a smile.

"What issue will the article be in?" asked Mrs. Pelton.

"Probably this next week's issue."

"Well, then I'll have to make sure we get the paper this week," she said to Marcia. Turning to me, she added, "Our delivery boy often forgets us."

I remembered the conversation with Shirley Peterson in the restaurant the other day. "Oh? If you're having a problem, maybe I can speak to someone about it."

"Could you? Boys will be boys, I'm sure, but it would be nice to receive the paper once in a while."

I put on my coat as footsteps came down the stairs. A young woman in her early twenties emerged from the foyer. She had long dark hair, bright brown eyes and an oval face. I knew at once that it was Rob's younger sister, Rose Pelton. Rose and I had been casual friends when I had experienced that glorious summer with Rob.

Rose stopped abruptly and stared at me. Then her full, dark red lips slid up into a smile of recognition. "Winnie? Winnie

Remington, is it really you?"

"Rose! How are you?"

Mrs. Pelton and Marcia both were surprised.

The girl stepped forward and embraced me, then stood with her hands on her hips. "Winnie, you look marvelous. Well, what are you doing here?"

I could feel myself blushing. "I'm with the newspaper. I'm writing an article on your family history."

"Oh, fun! But you're not leaving right now, are you?"

"Actually, I was."

Rose turned to her mother. "Mother, don't you remember Winnie?"

Mrs. Pelton studied me, but looked baffled. "You know, I thought when I first saw her she looked familiar, and her name seemed unusual."

Rose grinned. "*She's* the girl Rob went with in high school!"

Irene gasped. "Oh, is *that* who you are! Now I remember. But why didn't you say anything, dear?"

Marcia stared at me, an amused look in her eye. She didn't say anything. She just stood and smiled like a cat.

Rose continued to study me, still astonished. The last time I had seen Rose she had been just fourteen. She had grown into a very striking, attractive young woman. "Winnie, are you sure you can't stay?"

I wanted to. Oh, how I wanted to. "No, I couldn't. I've taken up enough of your mother's time," I said.

"Then you must come back sometime," Rose insisted. "Has Mother shown you some of the Pelton heirlooms?"

"Why, I never thought to get those old things out," replied Mrs. Pelton. "Would you care to see them? I could go through them this weekend."

I said I'd be thrilled to see them. We all headed into the foyer. I reminded them about the photographer coming by. As I walked to my car, I felt pleased with my success. I thought how proud Mr. Pendergast would be of me when I handed him my article on Monday.

What a stroke of luck to have Rose come in when she did. "Wait until JoAnn hears I've been invited back," I told myself as I got into my car and started up the engine.

During the drive home, I recalled more about Rose Pelton. Unlike Rob, Rose had been outgoing and popular. I remembered her as having lots of boyfriends, especially during my last year of high school, when Rose had been a freshman. She had an adventurous spirit and had been perhaps a little spoiled.

I had always admired Rose and ignored her shortcomings because her brother had been Rob. Later, I had learned from a circle of friends that Rose had quit high school because she was pregnant. I never learned the outcome, and now wasn't even sure it hadn't been just a rumor. During the summer months that Rob and I had dated, Rose had chatted with me several times when I had been over at the manor. I felt flattered that Rose remembered and had recognized me.

When I got home, I sat down and organized my notes from the manor. George came over, so I threw together a tossed salad and some ham sandwiches. I told him about my interview at the Peltons' that afternoon and found him to be impressed.

"You know, you've never done this much talking in a day, let alone one meal," said George.

I then noticed that most of my food was untouched. I had been going on and on all through supper and he was done and waiting for dessert. I laughed. "Am I really that bad?"

"I love it," he said.

I went to the counter and cut a piece of cherry pie for him. "Did you plan on us going anywhere tonight?" I asked.

"I didn't plan anything. But I did bring along the rest of the tests I didn't get corrected. These, by the way, are ones you can help me with."

"Oh, thrill." I set the pie plate and a clean fork down beside George.

"Mm, cherry pie is my favorite." He took a bite. "You bake a great pie, Fred."

While we corrected chemistry tests that evening, I couldn't

put Pelton Manor out of my mind. I remembered specifically that part of the conversation that had come up concerning Benjamin's death and Otto Pelton's stroke. I wondered what Rose knew and if I dared ask her about it.

After George left and I had gone to bed, I couldn't sleep. Thoughts swarmed through my head. I wondered about Rob, wondered if I would learn anything about him the next trip I made to the manor. Once I had thrived on any piece of information I could find about him, and I felt now like the impatient teenager I had once been.

While tossing and turning, trying to rid my restless head of all thoughts, I came up with an idea. I had toyed with the thought of going out for an early morning walk before the snow fell. I hadn't been out birding since summer, and I still had my nature column to write for next week's issue. Some fresh air might inspire fresh ideas. Why not go the next morning?

I almost called George to set up a dawn meeting place, but then figured George probably wouldn't go for such a last-minute crazy scheme. Although he accompanied me faithfully to Audubon meetings and seemed interested in the lectures and programs, field trips were a different matter. I always felt George preferred to stay home in a warm, soft bed, undisturbed.

7

A Gloomy Visit

SUNDAY MORNING I got up before dawn and threw together a small thermos of coffee, my binoculars and a field guide into the small backpack I always took when I went birding. It was freezing outside, but I had on my warmest gear, a down parka, down pants, a stocking cap and gloves. I felt like a stuffed sausage as I wedged myself into my car.

The first light of morning filtered through the haze on the eastern horizon as I drove down the deserted streets of Spundale toward the far side of town. My destination was the forest between the cemetery and Pelton Manor. By the time I crossed the railroad tracks, the heater in the car had warmed things up and I was actually sweaty. Of one thing I was certain, at least. I wouldn't have to worry about anybody seeing me like this. No other fool would be out this early on a Sunday morning.

Before heading into the woods, I decided to visit Alan's grave. I hadn't come in months. It wasn't that I despised cemeteries. On the contrary, I found a certain tranquility being there by myself. It was such a quiet, restful place where later in the day the sun would warm the rustling grasses and birds would chirp in the treetops.

I was reminded of the first yellow warbler I had ever seen. It had been right here in this cemetery. *Sweet, sweet, sweet, I'm so sweet!* it seemed to have sung. It saddened me to realize I'd have to wait six months to see any warblers.

Now the trees were bare, their naked limbs barely stirring in the cold November air. The sky was overcast and the cemetery had that dismal look often associated with death. The tombstones were fixed, skirted by brown leaves, unchanged and unchanging.

I wandered into the familiar lane where Alan's body lay. As I approached his marker, I noticed the copper name plate was no longer shiny. But his name was still legible:

ALAN WILLMORE GRANT

I huddled to keep warm. A mixture of feelings swept through me as I stood over his grave. Alan had been such a handsome young man, so full of ideas and the love of life. Together we had held so many plans. How difficult it was to think back upon the memories of that warm flesh-and-blood human being who had shared so many years alongside of me and then realize he was no more.

I had married Alan while we both were still in college. I finished my schooling, but Alan decided not to and got hired into his uncle's business. We had lived in the Detroit area for a while, but I longed to return to my beloved hometown of Spundale. So we bought the house on Willow Street and Alan did a lot of traveling for the company.

It was while he was on one of his business trips that the accident happened. And now, here I was without him. Strange. I could look back now without a single tear in my eye. Thinking back to last January, I had to wonder if I had exhausted all my sorrow in those difficult months that had followed. There had been feelings of anger as well as grief.

It had been late on a Saturday night last January when the police had called. They told me Alan had been in a car accident in Detroit. He died upon arrival at the hospital, along with the woman passenger who had been with him. Reports had shown the two had been drinking. I was to find out later that the excursion had been more than just a business trip. The woman passenger had been an ex-associate of Alan's and apparently they had been slipping off together on similar flings for quite some time. I had never suspected.

The wind came up suddenly and stirred tall brown grasses and withered leaves that had collected around Alan's gravestone. The pain was still there. I couldn't bring myself to weep, yet being there alone with my memories, I felt close to him. There had been a lot of happy times.

For a long moment it was silent and I was aware only of my breathing. Then, suddenly, a rustling noise startled me. I glanced to my right and saw a figure through the trees. A man in a red-and-black-checkered flannel jacket, wearing a cap with a bill, plodded out of the woods. I hadn't expected to see anyone out at this time of the day, but what caught my attention more was the long gun he carried at his side.

I decided to remain where I was until he left. Maybe he wouldn't see me. The man stopped at the edge of the cemetery and I saw him pull out a rag and run it across his forehead. Although I couldn't get a close look at his face, I did notice he had a beard. A jay in the trees above me rang out a series of distress squawks. I watched the man turn his face in my direction. Panic rose within me when he lifted his rifle and aimed right at me.

8

Encounter at Dawn

MY FIRST instinct was to make a mad dash for my car, but I had parked it near the road. Visiting Alan's grave had been on impulse. With my heart beating in my throat, I dodged behind the granite slab nearest me and crouched low. I waited for a shot to be fired. My breath billowed in visible wisps. After a minute, I peeked out to see what the man with the rifle was doing now.

He was no longer at the edge of the woods. I stood up and looked around. I caught a glimpse of red and black as a human figure fled toward the road. Whoever it was had gone. Maybe he hadn't been aiming at me. Perhaps he was a hunter—most likely a poacher since he wasn't wearing any blaze orange. Then, when he had seen a woman standing within firing range, he must have become alarmed and run off before I could identify and report him.

Sighing in relief, I headed in the opposite direction, into the woods. It was now fully daylight, although the sky was overcast and the sun didn't seem likely to appear. The woods surrounded me on all sides. I had always felt secure with trees around me. These trees, which were tall and gray with bare branches, felt especially comforting.

I cut through brush and brambles to reach the river. I remembered how I had felt when I had walked in these same woods before, with Rob. I could almost pretend he was beside me now, his hand in mine and his footsteps next to mine on the soft earth beneath dampened leaves and twigs.

My eyes and ears were alert for any signs of life. Once a squirrel scurried up a nearby tree trunk. Some black-capped chickadees scolded down at me from a spruce. They were practically the only birds I saw that morning, although I did hear a tufted titmouse call out, *Peter! Peter! Peter!* when I stood at the river's edge. I turned and walked deeper into the woods. After a while I found a stump to sit on. I pulled the thermos from my pack and poured some coffee. The hot drink warmed my fingers and took the chill out of my bones. Above the treetops I saw the sun trying to emerge through the clouds.

I thought of George. I recalled the little hints JoAnn and my friends had made. It seemed to be in everyone's mind that my destiny was to marry George Wyatt. It was the farthest thing from my mind, however. George did seem to be a good catch. He was quite the eligible bachelor, in fact. He was good-looking, intelligent, extremely gentle and thoughtful. I wondered what it was about George Wyatt that made me resist any ideas of a serious relationship.

Maybe he was just too nice, too friendly, too innocent. As much as I enjoyed his company and had even grown dependent on it, something was missing in our friendship. There was this lonesome kind of feeling inside me that George's companionship could not satisfy. I had hoped Alan could satisfy that feeling, but I had been mistaken.

I finished the last swallow of warm coffee and wondered if I should head back. I hadn't seen any birds worth seeing this morning, but my spirit felt renewed taking this time to come here by myself. My toes felt tingly from the cold, but I realized I wasn't far from the old mill. Before leaving the woods, I wanted to go there. I had fond memories of the old mill from the times Rob and I had walked there.

I packed up my thermos and started out. Dead leaves crunched beneath my feet as I made my way through rougher growth. Before long, I saw the roof of the mill through the trees and heard the quiet rush of water. Although the mill had been abandoned for years, the mill stream still fed the pond. The building itself was a ruin. Almost all the windows were smashed. The wooden boards were loose and faded.

I came within full view of the mill and stopped to rest. I remembered one hot afternoon when Rob had brought me here and we had gone for a dip in the pond. The place looked dreary now, so old and deserted. My toes and fingers were so cold they hurt. I thought I had better turn around.

Just then I realized I was not alone. A man was squatting on the weedy bank of the mill pond. I hadn't noticed him until now. His tan coat blended in well. He hadn't seen me. His back was toward me and the sound of the water had no doubt drowned the noise of my approach. He appeared to be deep in thought. I stood and stared for a long moment.

Then the man stood up and put his hands in his pockets. I drew in my breath. The man was Rob Pelton. I still couldn't see his face, but I knew it was him. It couldn't be anyone else. My heart pounded. I couldn't go to him. I didn't want to. Turning, I hoped to steal away into the woods unseen. Just as I did so, something stirred on the ground. With wings beating madly, a pheasant flew up in front of me. I was so startled, I fell to the ground, stunned.

Footsteps rushed up behind me and I looked up and met the equally startled expression on Rob's face. I didn't think I would ever forget that moment. I was too surprised to think about what I looked like, but I knew I must have been a sight in my down pants and parka with my nose bright red from the cold air.

"Are you all right?" asked that same gentle voice I remembered. Rob reached out his hand to help me up.

"I... I think so." I was surprised I was so calm. After all, I had never flushed a pheasant from its roost before. My eyes blurred. Rob was staring at me and I felt myself tremble.

"Winnie..." It was the same Rob, though ten years older.

I brushed myself off. "Hello, Rob." My voice rattled.

"It's really you?" He sounded perplexed. Then, suddenly he drew me close to him and I felt his chest against my chin. His arms were around me and I clung to him. I felt a surge of comfort in his arms. The next moment his grip loosened and he asked, "What are you doing here?"

I wanted to ask him the same thing. "I was... I was... on a walk."

"I never expected to see *you* in the woods," he replied. Glancing at the binoculars which dangled from my neck, he said, "What are you, some kind of a bird watcher?"

I confessed that I was. His smile told me he was pleased. I then remembered Rob had always held a great love for nature and the outdoors.

"I felt like a walk myself this morning," he explained. His voice became more relaxed as he studied me.

"But I thought... I mean, how..."

Rob smiled at me. "Actually, I just got into town this morning. I didn't feel like going to bed, and I didn't want to disturb anyone at the house." He shrugged.

Then we started walking. "Are you home for a visit?" I asked him.

"Yes." We walked in silence for a minute. Then he asked, "How have you been, Winnie?"

"Terrific." I was still too dazed by his sudden appearance to think of anything sensible to say.

When we came in sight of the manor, Rob said, "Do you need a lift anywhere?"

I explained that my car was parked at the cemetery.

"Oh," he replied.

We both stopped and stood, not looking at one another. I knew there were a million questions I wanted to ask him, but it was as if a sudden coldness or strangeness had come between us. Finally, I was too embarrassed to stand there any longer. I hadn't put on any makeup. I headed down the road toward the cemetery.

"Are you sure you're all right?" he asked.

"Yes." I kept walking.

"You're positive."

"Yes."

"Winnie, wait." I halted and let him catch up. "It was nice seeing you again. It's been a long time."

I swallowed. "Yes, it has been."

"Maybe... too long," he added with a sigh. I detected despair in his voice. at which he suddenly turned and walked up the hill toward the sleeping manor.

I couldn't bear another moment. I walked—almost ran—to my car. Once inside, I sat behind the steering wheel for a long time. I was aware of the sparrows chirping and a soft throbbing in my head.

I couldn't believe it. After ten years I had finally seen him, talked to him, even held him as in my fondest dreams.

But I felt so terribly alone. His words *too long* echoed in my brain. Finally, I slumped over the wheel and began to sob, first quietly, then louder until I couldn't control it. I cried hard and long, and then I stopped and started the ignition. It was getting late and I knew George might worry if he called and I wasn't there.

I took a hot shower when I got home. After a light brunch, the shock of seeing Rob had worn off enough so that I could think rationally again when George called early that afternoon. He came over and watched football while I sat at my laptop computer and composed *Nature Notes* for the week's issue. Then I began to peck out an article from my typed-up notes from Pelton Manor. It began to rain and the pattering of it on the roof was loud. For some reason, the monotonous sound of rain suited my mood and I completed my article and put it away before George's football game ended.

"Sorry I haven't been much company," George said. "Hey, let's go out for a pizza."

I sighed. "I don't feel like doing anything tonight, George."

"You okay, Fred? You've been quieter than usual today."

I explained about getting up early to go out birding.

"Actually, I'm quite tired. I think what I need is a nap."

George wasn't the least bit upset that I hadn't called him to go out in the woods with me that morning. He just grinned and told me good night, then left. Good old George. What a true friend.

I slept for an hour and then the telephone rang. It was still raining, I noticed, as I roused myself to pick up the phone. "Hello," I said groggily.

"Winnie!" It was a female voice, but I didn't know whose. "Hi, it's Rose Pelton."

I was surprised it was her. "Rose... hello."

"I found your number on the card you left with my mother. She wanted me to call and invite you to dinner. It will give her the opportunity to show you those heirlooms we were talking about."

I immediately perked up. Dinner at Pelton Manor! "Really? When?" I didn't know what else to say. Right away I wondered if Rob would be there. My heart began to race.

"Are you and your husband free tomorrow evening?" Rose asked.

I was seized with more of a surprise. For a moment I couldn't find my voice.

"Winnie, are you still there?"

"Uh, yes... my husband?" I finally said. I realized Rose probably didn't know I was a widow.

"Well, Mother said it was proper to invite both of you. Of course, if you'd rather come by yourself..."

I cleared my throat. "Rose, I've got to tell you. My husband was killed in a car accident almost a year ago."

There was a silence at the other end of the line. Then Rose gasped. "Oh, I had no idea! Oh Winnie, I'm terribly sorry. Nobody told me..."

I was used to this reaction by now and tried to comfort her. "Good heavens, Rose, how would you know? It's been years since we've seen each other."

"Why, I didn't even know you got married until yesterday,"

continued Rose. "I probably should have realized. Your name is Grant now. I'm so embarrassed."

"Well, don't be. I'd love to come over tomorrow evening for dinner."

"Oh, good. I'll tell Mother and Mrs. McCloskey. Is seven o'clock okay?"

"Seven's fine." I almost asked if Rob would be there. I wanted to mention to Rose how we had met at the mill that morning, but Rose seemed eager to end the conversation, probably since she had embarrassed herself. We said goodbye and I hung up with mixed feelings. Perhaps if I had said something about Rose's brother, it would sound as if I were trying to push my way back into his life, especially now that Rose knew I was widowed. Better to let events unfold by themselves, I decided. As much as I hoped to see Rob again, I couldn't forget the despair in his voice that morning when we had parted. What if he *didn't* want to see *me?*

9

Lunch with JoAnn

MR. PENDERGAST handed me the pages I had turned in Monday morning. "Take this to typesetting, Winifred. I didn't realize the Peltons had been so involved in starting our town."

"I may have more to write about after tonight," I revealed, and explained about the heirlooms Mrs. Pelton intended to show me.

"Fine, fine," said the boss. "Winifred, you're turning into a fine little reporter."

I was glad no one was around to have heard that remark.

Later, JoAnn and I had lunch together. We tied on our rain scarves as we walked down to the elevator. It had rained all night and was still drizzling slightly, putting everybody into a blue Monday mood.

"What did Mr. P. say about your article?" asked JoAnn.

"I think he liked it."

"How was your big date with George Friday night?"

Suddenly it seemed like Friday night was a year ago. So much had happened since then. "It was okay."

"You don't sound very enthused."

I pushed the button in the elevator and the doors closed. "We actually did have a great time," I insisted. "George even took me dancing."

"Well, next time maybe we can double," JoAnn suggested.

"I wanted to wait and tell you at the restaurant, but I can't wait. I've met the most marvelous man!"

"Who?"

"I'm sure you don't know him. He's a regular customer whose account I took over." The elevator stopped at the main floor and we got out. "I always wanted to mention him to you, but until this morning I wasn't really sure about him. And guess what? He finally asked me out!"

"JoAnn, that's great. Who is he?"

"A doctor."

"You're kidding."

"Actually, a psychologist."

I waited until we reached the car before I asked JoAnn again who it was.

"He's a very warm and caring person, Winnie. A decent man, for once, and age doesn't matter to us at all."

"Age?" I chuckled. "Jo, how much older is this guy?"

"I don't know his exact age. I didn't ask. But you'll see what I mean when you meet him. His name is Martin Spence."

When we got to the restaurant, JoAnn wanted to know the details of my interview at the Peltons', so I filled her in. "I met Mrs. Pelton's daughter-in-law, the one who married Benjamin. Her name's Marcia."

"Oh? What's she like?"

"I get the feeling when I'm around her that she's a cat and I'm a mouse."

JoAnn laughed. "Did you learn anything about Rob?" she asked eagerly. "Did they mention him at all?"

"No, and I didn't ask." I then explained how Rose had walked in just as I was leaving. "Actually, I'm surprised she remembered me. She knew me the minute she saw me. Mrs. Pelton didn't recognize me at all."

"Hm." JoAnn sipped her coffee. "What's she like now? Rose, I mean."

"She's got long dark hair. Rose is really a beauty, but you know she always was."

"Yes, and I suppose she's just as wild as ever too."

I thought JoAnn was being unfair. "No, I can't say for sure, Jo. People can change over the years." I almost added, "Alan and Jack did," but kept it to myself.

"Well, that's too bad they didn't tell you anything about Rob," JoAnn commented.

I wiped my lips with the napkin. "I saw him."

"What!" JoAnn stared through her huge glasses in disbelief. "You saw Rob? You mean, he was there as well? But you said…"

"No," I interrupted her, "this was yesterday." I then told her about my adventure in the woods Sunday morning and how I had stumbled across Rob at the old abandoned mill. "Apparently he was out for a walk, too."

"It's like…" JoAnn sighed. "Oh, Winnie, it's like the two of you were drawn to that one spot, like two stranded lovers out of a dream."

I couldn't tell if JoAnn was being facetious, or if she was really on my side. I could never tell those things with JoAnn. "I'm sure it was just a rare coincidence."

JoAnn asked me what I had found out about him during our meeting. "What does he do now?"

"I haven't the slightest idea."

When we got back from lunch, I indexed articles from last week's issue. It was the only duty I could concentrate on as I grew more and more nervous about the upcoming evening. I was all too glad when five o'clock arrived. This time the suspense of going over to the Peltons' was much greater. I knew Rob would be there. I longed to see him, to talk with him again, to find out answers to the things that had bothered me all these years. I wondered if tonight would be a turning point in my life.

10

Stormy Evening

IT CONTINUED to rain all day. When dusk settled in, I drove through town on my way to Pelton Manor. Rob was very much on my mind.

A few downstairs lights were on in the old house as I pulled into the driveway. Even inhabited, the place had an air of loneliness. The high windows looked especially black and forgotten. I turned off my windshield wipers, engine and headlights. The rain pattered down on my car.

The hired woman, Mrs. McCloskey, answered the bell this time and let me in. She returned my greeting with a smile, but I noticed a glint of uneasiness in the housekeeper's eye as she closed the door. "Miss Rosie is upstairs. I'll call her."

"No need for that," Rose called from the top of the stairs. She was dressed in black pants and a red puff blouse. "Hi, Winnie!" Rose grinned as she came down. Her long dark hair was gathered behind her neck and fastened with a red ribbon. Mrs. McCloskey took my damp coat and I followed Rose into the living room.

"My mother and Marcia went out, but they should be home soon."

I sat down on the couch. I couldn't help glancing around. I felt as though Rob would walk into the room any moment.

"So how've you been?" Rose sank into a cushioned chair and crossed her legs.

"Not too bad."

Rose seemed to sense my apprehension. "Can I get you a drink?"

"I'd like one." There was a tremble in my voice.

Rose got up and opened a cupboard at the bar. "What would you like?"

"A brandy will do." I was reminded of my father, who had brought me up with the notion that if I stuck with brandy, I'd be safe and sensible. After the way I had reacted Friday night with George and the Burgundy wine, I certainly didn't want to come across as a lush.

"Are we alone in the house?" I ventured.

Rose handed me my drink and settled back in her chair. "Yeah. You, me and Mrs. Mac. Why?"

I couldn't stand the suspense a moment longer. "I thought Rob might be here." I quickly explained how we had met outside the abandoned mill in the woods the day before. My cheeks burned and I took a sip of brandy.

Rose sat up straight. "Then you know. Rob came home—yesterday. He surprised us all. But he had to leave again."

I wasn't sure what she meant.

"He flew back to Connecticut this afternoon," Rose explained. "He couldn't stay." She studied me and then added, "I'm glad you got the chance to see him."

Connecticut? I didn't know what to say. Disappointment must have shown on my face. I took a swig of brandy and it burned on its way down. Not wanting to appear as ridiculous as I felt, I changed the subject. "Are you living at home now?"

"Just temporarily." Rose took a sip of her drink. "I'm looking for a place of my own."

"But don't you like living in this elegant house?"

Rose sighed. "I just want to be on my own for a while."

I smiled. "I can understand what you mean. Did you go to college?"

"No, school was never my style." Rose pulled out a pack of cigarettes. "I've traveled around a lot since I got out of

50

high school. That's been my education, I suppose." She lit her
cigarette and drew a puff. Then her face turned somber and her
voice more tender. "Tell me, Winnie, was it ... *hard?*"

I knew she referred to my widowhood. "I'm managing."

"It must have been difficult for you."

"Well," I sighed, "it was hard for me at first."

"We don't have to talk about it, if you don't want to."

"No, I don't mind." I then told Rose about Alan's accident,
his affair, the whole mess. "Luckily, my parents were there
when I needed them," I concluded. "They had just retired
and sold their house and were in the process of moving to
the Southwest. They stayed with me awhile, and then I went
with them on a vacation to Hawaii. When I got back, I started
working at the newspaper. I started meeting new people, and
suddenly I didn't have time to feel sorry for myself anymore."

Rose relaxed, cigarette in hand, and stared off toward the
ceiling as she exhaled a cloud of smoke. "It had to be rough. It's
certainly been rough in *this* house the last few months."

I paused. Finally I asked, "What happened to Benjamin?"

Rose sighed. "To tell you the truth, Winnie, I really don't
know. I just don't know what happened to him that night."
I was startled and Rose could see that I was. "You see," she
continued, "I wasn't home last May when it happened. I was in
Colorado, on a motorcycle trip with this guy. I didn't find out
about his death until two days after it happened."

"Oh, Rose..."

"I was pretty upset when the state cops stopped us. I called
home right away and Mother wired some money for me to fly
home."

"Well, what do *they* say happened?" I asked.

Rose stood up and paced the floor. "They say he fell down
the stairs. It was dark and he got home late. He didn't turn on
any lights because he apparently didn't want to wake anyone.
Then my father heard him fall and got up and found him at the
bottom of the staircase."

I puzzled over this in my mind as I finished my brandy and

Rose squished out her cigarette butt in an ash tray.

"Then my father collapsed from a stroke," Rose added. "That's the word of Mother and Marcia. They were the only ones in the house when it happened. Except Dad, of course." She stood up, walked over to the fireplace and picked up a picture frame. She turned back to me. "Anyway, the story sounds plausible enough. It *could* have happened that way, but for some stupid reason I just don't buy it."

"What does Rob think?"

Rose told me Rob had been in Connecticut and had come home after hearing the news. "He has no trouble buying their story," she commented.

"So what do you think *really* happened?" I was almost afraid to ask.

Rose shrugged. "I don't know. I can halfway believe that Ben's death was accidental, but not my father."

I sat up straight on the edge of the couch. "Rose, how long did your father live after his stroke?"

"Well, as soon as Ben's funeral was over and Dad was no longer critical, my mother had him committed to a rest home. You may have heard of it, the Spider Lake Resort."

I nodded.

Rose went on. "Mother was positive it was the best thing for him. Rob and I both tried to talk her into keeping him here at the manor and hiring a live-in nurse. She almost gave in, but at the last minute she changed her mind and made the arrangements with Spider Lake."

"But why so far away?"

"It's the highest rated rest home in the Lower Peninsula," said Rose, "and cost was certainly no barrier. Mother was sure he would recover faster there." Rose fought to keep her voice steady as moisture filled her brown eyes. She hugged the picture of her father to her breast. "Dad died up at Spider Lake about a month later. It was such a shock to me—to all of us, really—because we were so sure he was getting better. The doctors had said he had a fifty percent chance of a complete recovery from the paralysis."

I sat in silence as Rose replaced the picture frame, then drew out another cigarette. My stomach rumbled from hunger. Whatever was cooking from elsewhere in the manor smelled wonderful.

"Hey, how long has it been since you and Rob went together?" Rose asked as she lit another cigarette.

"Ten years."

Rose blew out a cloud of smoke. "Did you know Rob was in Connecticut?"

"No, not until this week. Up to now I had no contact with him." I hoped I didn't sound resentful.

"He was offered a professorship last spring," Rose explained.

"So he teaches?"

"Sometimes."

"He used to talk about becoming a doctor," I remembered.

"Oh, he gave up that dream and went into biological research. We keep in touch. He never comes home much, though. Usually he calls or I telephone him at least once a week. Winnie, would you like his number?"

I drained my glass. Of course I wanted Rob's phone number. I envisioned myself getting in touch with him and wondered how it would be, especially after our meeting at the mill. But the pain from the old wound that had opened up began to throb. I sighed and shook my head. "It's been such a long time, Rose. I really think if Rob had wanted our relationship to continue, he would have done something about it."

"Are you sure?" Rose prompted. It was getting extremely hot in the room all of a sudden. Rose watched me carefully. I thought she was on the verge of giving me his number anyway, but at that moment we heard voices in the foyer. The front door shut and Mrs. McCloskey's voice dominated the rest.

"Here, let me take those wet things from you, ma'am. What? Raining still? Haven't we had enough of this nasty weather?"

Rose took a last puff from her cigarette, then extinguished it.

Irene Pelton entered from the foyer, followed by Marcia. "I hope we haven't been keeping dinner waiting. Hello, Winnie, how are you, dear?"

"Quite fine, thank you."

Marcia untied a scarf from her head and exposed dampened blonde tresses. She eyed me calmly without a word of greeting.

Mrs. McCloskey served a delicious dinner. Afterward, we sat around with coffee while Rose helped the housekeeper bring in dessert.

"So you're a widow Rose tells me," Marcia remarked.

"Yes." I tilted the coffee cup to my lips.

"We have something in common then," Marcia resumed. She gave a little toss to her blonde hair. "Well, after some time passes, we all adjust." There was a hint of sarcasm in her voice. "Tell me, how long did you know Rob?"

I explained how I had known him briefly in high school, smiled politely, but offered nothing more.

Marcia took another sip of her coffee. "No, I meant how long did it *last?*"

I could feel my pulse rising. I couldn't tell this stranger that it had never ended—for me, at least. What concern was it of hers, anyway? She certainly had a lot of nerve asking such a thing.

"Actually," I began...

"Dessert!" Rose cut me off as she and Mrs. McCloskey carried in four peach parfaits. I was only too glad not to have to continue with Marcia's line of questioning.

Outside the rain came down harder. There were flashes of lightning and distant rumblings of thunder. We commented on the storm as we ate our dessert. Then Irene Pelton remembered the reason for my visit.

"I'm sure you're eager to see some of those heirlooms," she said. "Would you care to tour the manor?"

"I'd like to very much."

After the dishes were cleared away, Irene led me through the dining room to the foyer. Down a hallway we came to a room elegantly decorated, filled with books, which was obviously the library. As we crossed into the parlor, a grand piano in the corner caught my eye. "What a beautiful piano," I commented. "Does anyone play?"

"Benjamin did," said Irene. "Benjamin was a very talented child. That boy was mastering Beethoven at the age of ten." She sighed. "Oh, the memories that come to mind when I look at that old piano and think of the many recitals he was in."

"Didn't Rob and Rose play as well?"

"Well, yes, I suppose they fooled around a little." I got the impression that it didn't matter to her how well her other children played. It was obvious that Benjamin had been Irene's favorite.

We toured the rest of the first floor, including a room which had been decorated in red and black with paneled walls and a billiard table. "This was my late husband's den. Otto, my husband, used to spend a lot of his time in this room." She pointed out two small bedrooms near the kitchen, which had once been used as servants' quarters. Mrs. McCloskey slept in one of them and the other was vacant.

We climbed the staircase to the second floor, which consisted of six huge rooms. Irene took me briefly through each bedroom, and lingered in the one Benjamin had slept in as a boy.

"Everything is just as it was when he was young," Irene murmured. I stood at the door while the older woman roamed around the room and touched things and fluffed the pillows on the bed. She had ordered that none of the things in Benjamin's room be removed or stored away, I later learned from Rose.

Eager to see the third floor, I inquired about it. Irene shook her head. "We no longer use that part of the house," she replied. "With just the three of us living in this big house, it's ridiculous to pay for the heating of the third floor. There are five more rooms upstairs, but we have boarded them up. Besides, it's unsafe."

"Why is it unsafe?" I asked.

"There are loose floorboards and such. At one time the roof

leaked horribly." As we walked past the narrow stairway that led to the third floor, I lingered and looked up at the darkness. Irene turned and noticed me. "Winnie?" she called.

Reluctantly, I followed her into the next room.

"Didn't you ever see the house before?" Rose asked me later, when we were alone in Rose's room on the second floor.

"No, not all of it. In fact, not much of it." I explained that Rob and I had not spent much time at the manor that summer we had dated. Rose's room was lavender, the walls smeared with posters, and an old stereo was against one of the walls. It was an adolescent's room. A door led into a private bath that was shared with the adjoining bedroom. Rose motioned for me to sit on her bed and she got out a photo album. A crash of thunder made us jerk. The storm seemed to be getting worse.

"There are some pictures of Rob in here, if you'd like to see them." Rose handed me the album. Suddenly, I felt ten years younger, as if Rose and I were schoolgirls sharing secrets in Rose's room. I paged through the album while Rose related to me a few of her adventures. I pieced two and two together and figured out that it was true Rose had left high school. Whether the reason was because she had gotten pregnant or not, Rose didn't say—and I didn't ask.

Another flash of lightning and a crash of thunder. I concentrated once again on the photo album and finally found a recently taken snapshot of Rob. He looked much the same as he had yesterday morning at the mill, which was how he had looked ten years ago. It was amazing. I had always figured men were the ones who aged faster. The wavy auburn hair was thick over his head and he had sideburns. He was standing in front of what looked like a new sports car.

A crackle of thunder, topped with a triple flash of lightning, suddenly seemed to grip the very walls of the old house. Then everything was in complete darkness. Rose gave a startled cry. I let the photo album drop onto the bed and jumped to my feet. From downstairs we heard Marcia call out, "What happened?"

A woman screamed from somewhere in the house. I felt

Rose rush past me into the hall. "Mrs. McCloskey!" she cried.

I reached my hands out and felt along the cold, smooth walls into the hallway.

"Rose?" Irene Pelton called from downstairs.

"We're all right, Mother."

Mrs. McCloskey sobbed in the background. Marcia tried to calm her, but the housekeeper's cries continued. Another flash of lightning brightened the hallway from the front window, followed by an ear-shattering blast of thunder. I cringed and clutched the staircase rail.

"Wait here. I've got a flashlight in my room," said Rose. "I'll get it." She groped her way back into the bedroom.

I looked up at the stairway which led to the third floor. Suddenly, I no longer cared to go up there. How frightening it was to stand there alone with the drone of rain and thunder and lightning. It was as if I were in some horror movie. Then I looked down the staircase and realized I might be standing at the very spot where Benjamin Pelton had plunged to his death.

"I'm coming, Winnie," Rose called out. A minute later she emerged with a beam from her flashlight. We started down the steps together. Mrs. McCloskey clucked excitedly in the next room.

Irene met us at the bottom of the stairs holding a candle she had lit. "I do hope the lights won't be out too long," she said.

"I don't like this place, I don't like it," Mrs. McCloskey whimpered, "especially when something like this happens. I just don't like this place at all, Mrs. Pelton."

Rose stepped over to put her arm around the housekeeper. "You're not afraid of the dark, are you, Mrs. Mac?"

"It ain't the dark that worries me," cried Mrs. McCloskey. "No, Miss Rosie, it what's *in* the dark."

"Oh, there's nothing to be afraid of," Rose consoled her. "We're all here with you now."

"I know that, Miss Rosie." Mrs. McCloskey's trembling voice rose in pitch. "We're *all* here. I can feel the presence—all of us and all of *them!*"

11

The Drive Home

THE LIGHT from Irene's candle flickered in the dim hallway. Outside the rain continued to pound against the timeworn walls of the manor.

"What's she talking about?" snapped Marcia. "Tell her to stop that foolish talk!"

Mrs. McCloskey whimpered louder. "I can't help it. I can't!" sobbed the housekeeper.

"Pay no attention," Irene chided as we all moved into the parlor and took seats. A few minutes later, the lights flickered and then came on again.

"Thank heaven." Mrs. McCloskey clutched her heart. "I hope that's the worst of it." Her eyes were red and swollen from crying.

Marcia drew a curtain aside and glanced out one of the Victorian windows. "The rain seems to be subsiding."

"Good." I stood up. "It's best that I start for home."

"Oh, don't go yet!" protested Rose. "Wait a little longer, please."

"We hate to think of you driving home in this rain," added Irene.

Marcia let the curtain fall back. Mrs. McCloskey wiped her eyes, then went back into the kitchen to finish cleaning up.

"Stay a little longer, dear," coaxed Irene. "It's so nasty out."

"It's not late," said Rose. She led me into the library. "Poor

Mrs. McCloskey. After tonight, I doubt if she'll stay with us the rest of the week like she promised."

"Why? What's wrong?"

"She doesn't like this house." Rose lit a cigarette. I sat down and waited for Irene and Marcia to follow us in, but they didn't come. "She just hates living here," Rose added.

"How come?"

"She's very superstitious. She claims she has psychic abilities. Once she insisted she saw a man at the top of the stairs when she was taking up some linens. She nearly had a heart attack."

"Was anyone else home?" I asked.

"No, she was alone. Mother had just come back from somewhere and heard her cry out."

"Well, did she actually see someone, or was it just her imagination?"

"Who knows? It happens a lot with her, I guess. She's only been with us a month. She says she can't stand living in this house, that she can feel a presence."

"It's enough to give one the creeps." I shuddered.

Rose laughed. "I know a couple of creeps you might be interested in talking to." She tapped her cigarette on an ash tray. "My great-aunts live in the lane behind the property. They'll tell you the manor is haunted." Then she laughed. "I'm really putting you on. I'm sorry, Winnie. Aunt Ophelia and Aunt Pearl are my father's aunts. They're two sisters who never got married. Actually, they're the sweetest two old ladies I know."

"Do they know a lot about your family history?" I grew interested at the idea of writing a follow-up article for the *Focus* column.

"Oh sure, but I'll warn you. They talk incessantly."

"Maybe I'll pay them a visit this week."

Irene entered the library then. "If you'll excuse me, I think I'll retire early tonight. Winnie, I hope you'll come back to see us again soon. We've enjoyed having you."

I stood up. "Thank you, Mrs. Pelton. Dinner was excellent. I really should be going now."

Rose made no protest as she followed me into the foyer.

"Thanks for inviting me," I told them.

"You're most welcome," said Irene. "The paper comes out on Thursday, am I right?"

"Yes." Rose found my coat.

"Well, I certainly hope the boy delivers it this time."

"I'll see to it," I assured her.

After the good-nights were said, I dashed out into the rain to my car. The air felt fresh and cold with the lingering odor of earthworms. The rain was letting up, I noticed, as my car rolled down the sloping drive. I yawned and suddenly felt worn out as my mind went over the evening's events. I was intrigued by Mrs. McCloskey's claim of feeling a presence in the manor, and wanted to find out more about what she alleged to have seen on the stairs. Rose had appeared as happy-go-lucky as when I had known her ten years ago, except for her dire concern over her father's and brother's deaths. Why did she feel there was more to it than what they had told her?

Suddenly I was aware of blinding headlights in my rear-view mirror. I was crossing the railroad tracks toward the more populated section of Spundale. I didn't recall when the car behind me had started following me, but it seemed too close and it had its brights on. In annoyance, I tried adjusting my rear-view mirror and made a left turn. The car behind me also made the left turn.

I had expected to see Rob tonight at the manor, but he was back in Connecticut. I wondered if I would ever see him again. My second chance had come and gone yesterday morning, I realized with regret.

Another left turn and I was convinced now that someone was following me. I couldn't imagine who or why. I decided to go out of my way. I led the tailer through back streets of unfamiliar neighborhoods. Sure enough, the car followed everywhere I went. I began to panic. It was late on a week night, and not a lot of cars were on the road. I didn't want to risk leading some psycho to my isolated street. At the same time, I was tired and had to work tomorrow. I couldn't cruise the streets of Spundale all night long.

At the next corner I slowed, pulled over to the side, then whirled my car around in a U-turn and sped away in the opposite direction. I'd drive over to George's house if that car was still following me. But as I approached the next stoplight and dared to glance in my mirror, I saw that I had lost him. There was no car following me now.

It was barely drizzling by the time I pulled into my driveway. It had been an interesting and eventful evening, but I couldn't wait to hit my pillow. I would have no trouble going to sleep this night.

12

The Cottage in the Lane

THE SUN came out Tuesday morning. If it had been spring, everything would have looked green and alive after the extended weekend rain. Instead, the autumn leaves lay withered and brown along wet curbs and gutters. The trees looked even more naked than before. The bitter promise of a Michigan winter could be felt in the chilled air.

JoAnn had a luncheon appointment with a client, so I ate alone in a downtown café. I wondered if I would ever go back to Pelton Manor. The more I thought about it, the more I realized there was no reason to go back.

I took a sip of coffee and suddenly felt depressed and empty. It was over—the only chance I'd had to see Rob Pelton again —and I had been foolish to hope this assignment could lead to anything more than a human interest story for the *Spundale Star*.

I didn't feel ready to return to work after I paid for my lunch and left the café. I wanted to be alone in a place where I had found refuge before, when my life had been down in the dumps. I got into my car and drove to the cemetery near Pelton Manor.

The sun was out all the way. The cemetery was peaceful, secluded by trees and headstones. I sat in my car with the window rolled down and listened to the wind and watched the sway of bare branches. A small flock of sparrows twittered and foraged in the grasses.

Eventually thoughts about last evening crept into my mind. I recalled Rose telling me I should pay a visit to the two great-aunts. Their cottage was in the lane behind the manor. I could leave my car parked in the cemetery and walk to their house.

I rolled up the window and locked the doors, then headed toward the manor. The cottage the Pelton aunts lived in was small and quaint, surrounded by trees and beds of autumn flowers that were turning brown now after the frost. Shrubs and hanging pots lined the front porch. I followed a cobblestone path to the front door. A small terrier began yipping from inside as I approached. The front door opened, and an old woman peeped out at me.

"Who is it?" called a voice from inside the cottage.

"Hello," the old woman called to me. "May I help you?"

"My name is Mrs. Grant. I'm a friend of Rose," I explained, "Rose, your niece, up at the manor."

The woman stepped out of the cottage, where I could see her completely. "Oh, a friend of Rose." She was small with gray hair pulled back into a bun. Her face was wrinkled and her tiny brown eyes reminded me of a bird's. When she smiled, I noticed a gold filling. "Won't you come in, then?"

The dog lunged forward and I instinctively drew back. The woman snatched him by the collar. "No, no! Here!" she chided. "Inside, you. He doesn't take to strangers, I'm afraid."

"Who is it, Pearl?" the voice inside called again.

I followed the woman into the cottage. I found myself standing in a cozy living room that smelled of lavender. Something delicious was baking in the kitchen. The furniture was simple, with plenty of crocheted afghans and seat covers. Lace curtains, slightly faded from sunlight, hung at the window.

"It's a friend of Rose," the small woman called out.

A moment later, the other aunt appeared from the kitchen. She was a little taller, with white hair pinned back into braids wrapped tightly on top of her head. Drying her hands on a towel, she smiled cordially. "Oh, how nice to have company on such a lovely day."

"Sister, I'd like you to meet Mrs. Grant."

"Please call me Winnie."

The white-haired woman extended her hand. "I am Rose's Aunt Ophelia," she said, "and you have already met her Aunt Pearl."

The terrier sniffed at my feet. When I bent down to pet him, the animal backed away.

"Here! Here!" scolded Pearl.

"He's such a nuisance," added Ophelia, "but he won't bite."

"Please sit down," said Pearl.

"I hope I'm not disturbing you," I said.

"Not at all. We've been baking," said Ophelia. "Do you like banana bread?"

So *that* was the heavenly smell. "Yes," I replied, then explained, "The reason I came by was to talk to you about family history." I then told them about the article I was doing for the paper. Both ladies' eyes lit up with interest.

"We'd be happy to tell you anything you want to know," said Pearl.

"You look a bit old to be a friend of Rose," mentioned Ophelia. She seated herself in an antique rocker that creaked when it moved.

"Now sister," scolded the gray-haired aunt, "Rose is no longer a little girl, you know."

"Yes, yes, I know." The rocker creaked steadily.

"Actually," I confessed, "I'm more of an old friend of Rob." I detected sudden looks of knowing in both old ladies' eyes as they nodded at each other and smiled.

"It's been a long time since we've seen Robby," remarked Ophelia.

"Since last August," murmured Pearl.

"Oh, before that," said Ophelia. "It was Otto's funeral in July."

"Oh heavens." A short silence followed and then Pearl asked, "You know about our nephew Otto, don't you?"

"Poor Otto," said Ophelia. She drew a handkerchief out of her apron pocket and dabbed at her eyes.

"Yes, I know about him," I replied softly.

"And poor Benjamin." Ophelia moaned.

Pearl's beady eyes were moist too, as she asked, "What did she tell you about the dear boy?"

I hesitated. "Who do you mean?"

"Why, Irene, of course. What did she tell you happened to him that night?"

"Now, Pearl, I don't think Mrs. Grant would be interested in our theory." Ophelia blew her nose into the handkerchief.

I sat on the edge of my chair. Ophelia composed herself, and then she was the one who started to explain about the *theory*.

"It was no accident that Benjamin fell down those stairs," she said. "He was *pushed.*"

Although alarmed at her words, I sat calmly and waited to hear the rest.

"That's right," continued Pearl. "We're sure he was murdered."

I kept a straight face. "Murdered? Who would do such a thing?"

"It was one of three persons who must have done it," said Ophelia.

Pearl broke in. "It could have been Marcia. We pretty much agree it had to be Marcia, don't we, sister?"

Ophelia nodded in agreement. "She and Benjamin were having difficulties," she explained, "you know, with their marriage."

"I wasn't aware of that."

"Oh yes," insisted Pearl, "they were married only a few months."

"And, of course, Irene was totally against the marriage before it ever took place," added Ophelia.

"She loathed Marcia," cried Pearl.

"Marcia wasn't exactly up to Irene's standards," Ophelia

explained. "You see, she grew up on the wrong side of the tracks, so to speak."

"Taking her favorite son away from her was reason enough for Irene," put in Pearl.

"But Mrs. Pelton seems to be very fond of Marcia." I remembered how close the two of them had seemed both times I had seen them together. "Besides, why would Marcia want to kill her husband?"

"Who knows what motive she had?" said Pearl. "The main thing is she did it. She pushed Benjamin down the stairs and he died. If she didn't, well... *some*body did!"

"But how can you be so sure?" I challenged.

"We have no proof whatsoever." Ophelia sighed.

"But we know by the way things have changed over in the manor that Benjamin's death was no accident," said Pearl.

"That's right," agreed her sister.

"How do you mean? What's changed?"

"Now you'll really think we're crackers," said Ophelia. "Why, the ghost, of course."

Pearl rolled her eyes. "Yes, the ghost. You see, the manor is now inhabited by one."

I recalled Rose's remark last night about how the aunts believed the manor was haunted. I pretended to be alarmed by the news. I didn't dare smile.

"That's why Pearl and I try to manage by ourselves as best we can. We prefer not to go near that place, if at all possible."

"Did you see a ghost?" I asked.

"Oh no, no, no. We haven't seen anything yet," said Ophelia.

"But we know it's there, just the same," said Pearl.

"Have you told anyone about your theory?" I noticed the terrier was now asleep at my feet.

"Oh yes, we've told everyone," said Pearl, "the police... Irene..."

"And everybody thinks we're a little crazy upstairs." Ophelia laughed and pointed to her temple. "I think the banana bread is done." She rose and went into the kitchen.

Pearl's expression was still serious, but I could tell her mind had completely dismissed the subject when she said, "I forgot to call the egg man this morning. Mrs. Howard wanted me to order a dozen eggs for her."

"He usually has an extra dozen with him," Ophelia called from the kitchen.

I noticed a wall clock with a swaying pendulum and suddenly realized how late it was getting. I was on an extended lunch hour and wondered if they needed me back at the office. "Do you mind if I use your telephone?" I asked.

"Please go ahead." Pearl showed me where it was.

Marion answered right away. "Marion, it's Winnie. Are you swamped?"

"Hardly."

I asked if Mr. Pendergast was in.

"No, he went to a council meeting."

I explained that I was on an interview. "If you think you need me..."

"No, I can handle things here," Marion assured me. "Oh! Before you hang up, someone came by to see you—a Mr. Wyatt."

I sighed. "Oh yes. Did he say what he wanted?"

"No." I figured George had probably dropped in just to say hello. I thanked Marion and hung up. It was rare that I took afternoons off, but I remembered Mr. Pendergast had said I should take as much time as I wanted to fill in for Sara.

I spent the rest of the afternoon in the company of the two great-aunts. I was more entertained by their recollections and references to their ancestors than I was willing to record in my notes.

Nothing more was said about the old ladies' theory. The dinner hour was approaching when I was finally able to escape from their hospitality. They invited me to stay for supper, but I had to convince them I had already taken up enough of their time.

"Oh nonsense," Ophelia pouted.

Then Pearl appeared from the kitchen with a loaf of banana

bread, wrapped in aluminum foil. She held it out to me.

"Oh no, I couldn't."

"Please take it," said Pearl. "I made a double batch." Smiling sweetly, she tucked the loaf into my arms.

I thanked them and started out into the early darkness.

"Where is your car?" asked Ophelia.

I explained that it was parked over at the cemetery.

"What a lovely day it turned out to be," commented Pearl, "and after all that rain."

"You must come back and visit us again soon," called Ophelia.

As I walked down the lane with the bundle of banana bread under my arm, I realized it was later than I had anticipated. It was almost dusk. Such sweet old ladies, but so funny. At least they had cheered me up. I no longer felt as depressed as before. How weird it had been, though, when they talked about Benjamin's death. I wondered if they really believed someone had deliberately pushed him down the stairs. It didn't seem likely. I was sure their overactive imaginations were responsible for cooking up such possibilities.

The breeze felt refreshing. It reminded me of my outing the other morning and how the day had been dawning, just as the day was coming to an end now. I could see the orange and pink sky behind the treeline as the manor towers came into view. The memory of seeing Rob was still vivid in my mind.

A snapping twig startled me and I stopped. Glancing around, I saw that nothing was there. Then, deciding it was only a squirrel, I continued toward the cemetery. I took a deep breath of air. The smell of late autumn brought the crisp odor of smoking leaves from somewhere. I thought back to my childhood with a trace of nostalgia as the image of my father, rake in hand, burning a pile of leaves, flashed into my mind. Nowadays I resented the idea of anybody polluting the environment by such an act.

A noise through the bushes caused me to glance to my left. Something was there. What? I waited a moment. If it was a small animal or a bird, I wanted to see it. I started toward the bushes, expecting the creature to flee from my presence. When nothing happened, I shrugged and continued on my way. The light was growing dimmer.

The next time the brush rustled, I felt a chill race through me. Something or someone was following me. I had that strange feeling that I was definitely not alone. I was still about halfway between the aunts' cottage and my parked car at the cemetery. If I let on that I knew someone was following me, would I be accosted?

Adrenalin surged and I started to run. The fight-or-flee instinct had gripped me and I didn't question my choice. I ran as fast as I could, grateful to be wearing flats instead of my heels. I didn't look behind me.

By the time I reached my car, I was panting and could feel my heart pounding. I found the car keys in my purse and soon had the door open. I fell into the driver's seat and felt like the world was spinning before my eyes. There was no rapist waiting to get me outside the car. No one was there now. Maybe I had imagined it all.

As my breathing slowed and my heart calmed, I saw it was almost dark. The banana bread was squished on one end. I laid it on the passenger's seat and then started up the engine. When I pulled into my driveway, I noticed George's car already there.

"Another five minutes and I was going to call the police." George smiled in relief as I climbed out and we walked to the house together.

"I'm sorry," I said, "I didn't know you'd be waiting for me."

"I left a message at the paper. Where were you?"

I unlocked the door and stepped inside. "I was visiting a couple of very nice old ladies."

"Another interview?"

"Yes." I turned on the kitchen light. For some reason I was annoyed at George. I felt I didn't have to explain anything to him.

"Well, I couldn't help being a little worried, Fred. It's dark. I didn't want anything to happen to you."

I shuddered as I remembered the noise in the bushes. I was positive someone had been following me after I left the Pelton sisters' cottage.

"Hey, is everything all right?" asked George. "You seem a little on edge."

"No, I'm fine."

"Are you sure?"

"Of course I'm sure. Will you excuse me for a few minutes? I have to get out of these clothes." Without waiting for a reply, I scampered down the hall to my bedroom and closed the door. I was mad at myself for acting this way, but I couldn't help it. I changed into something more casual and brushed my hair, taking my time.

Thoughts about Rob filtered through my mind. Had it actually been a coincidence he had been at the mill the other morning? Perhaps there were forces beyond our understanding that had brought the two of us together again. Was it destiny? Then why had he left?

"Fred?" George called from the living room. I hung up my dress and joined him. "Are you sure everything's all right?" he asked. "You're acting a little strange."

"I am?"

"Don't take offense."

"I'm not."

"It's just that I... well, I happen to care about you." He smiled and I saw something in those boyish blue eyes that made my heart skip a beat.

"I'm okay... really." I smiled back.

He sighed. "Well, I won't probe. Hey, how about seeing a movie tonight? There's a new one in town that's supposed to be pretty good."

"I don't feel like a movie."

"Well, okay. What would you like to do?"

I sat down. "Actually, nothing."

George sat down next to me. "Did you have a bad day?"

"Not especially." I felt him put his hand on my knee and it startled me. After all, it wasn't like George to try anything.

"I can see something's bugging you." When I said nothing, he continued, "Are you just going to sit there the rest of the evening and not talk to me?"

I turned and met the gentle sympathy in his eyes. For a second I flickered a smile, but then I recalled the similar look in Rob's brown eyes when he had helped me to my feet the other morning. I had to turn away.

"Fred, please. Let's talk. Now I know something is wrong. I can sense it. Are you mad at me?"

"No, George, of course not." Why was I feeling so uptight?

"I thought we could talk to each other," he pressed.

I started examining my fingernails. "I'd rather not talk right now, George."

"Why not?"

"It's too... because it's personal."

He stretched out his legs and folded his arms. Then he let out a big sigh. "It has something to do with those articles you're writing, doesn't it?" His voice had lost its softness.

"A little," I confessed. I felt my eyes start to swell with moisture. I didn't know why I was getting so worked up.

George sighed. "Okay, so you're under stress. The boss has you doing double duty. I know it must be hard on you, having to gather all that information. It can't be fun going to strange people's houses and asking them all sorts of questions."

I swallowed to compose myself. "I don't mind it, really."

"But it's not like you're going to be doing it full-time," he said. "You're done writing those articles now, aren't you? It's *over*."

I realized then why I was so depressed. George had said it—it was *over!* Seeing Rob again—and losing him again. I would never get another chance. My lip quivered. How could my life ever be the same now? After dreaming of it all these years, I had finally seen Rob Pelton again, only to lose him

71

before any of my questions could be answered. A sob broke loose. Embarrassed, I buried my face in my hands.

"Fred, what's wrong?"

Then the tears began rolling down my cheeks. I couldn't help it. I felt so humiliated to be crying in front of George. He tried to comfort me by putting his arm around me.

"Don't!" I sobbed as I tried to break loose.

"Come on, Fred, let it out. You'll feel better."

"You don't understand." I pulled away from him. "I'm so mixed up."

"But I think I do understand." He reached for me again.

"Don't!" The sobs still came. He tried to hold me and brushed tears from my cheek with his hand. Indignant, I stood up to get away from him. "George, please! Just leave me alone!"

Through the blur of tears, I saw the shock in his bewildered expression. I suddenly hated myself for being so mean to someone who had tried to be my friend. I wanted to apologize, but sobs choked me and I could only bury my face in shame. I was aware of him getting up and slipping on his jacket. Then, he sauntered out and I heard the door close quietly behind him.

13

An Apology

LATER THAT evening, I tried to call JoAnn, but apparently she had gone out. I felt troubled by the scene I had caused with George, and more troubled by thoughts of despair over my encounter with Rob in the woods. I needed someone to talk to.

Why had Rob returned to Spundale only to leave again? Perhaps it was on my account. He had seemed happy to see me, though. I had experienced that much, hadn't I? Holding me the way he had, even briefly, I was sure he must still love me. My mind went over and over the scene until I had myself ninety-nine percent convinced I had no reason to feel hurt. Yet I still did. Rob had said *too long*. He had said it as if it was too late for us now, or ever. Most likely, I knew, there was someone else in his life back in Connecticut.

I finally gathered up the nerve to call George just before I went to bed. I could tell by his voice when he answered that he had already been sleeping.

"Hello," came the muffled voice on the other end.

"George? Did I wake you?"

"Winnie!" At once he perked up.

"I just wanted to apologize for the way I acted. You're not mad, are you?"

George was grinning. I could tell. "Of course not. I'm glad you're feeling better."

"I felt so ashamed after you left. I can just imagine what you must think of me."

"Don't say that. I'm glad you called, Fred. I was feeling pretty down. But I feel on top of the world now." He suggested we get together again tomorrow night and I consented. After we talked a couple of minutes longer, we said good-night and hung up.

I went right to bed, but I didn't sleep for a long time. I lay awake, remembering Rob, and feeling as if the old wound had been opened and rubbed with salt.

14

A Startling Surprise

LUCKILY, THERE were enough things to keep me busy at work the next day. There was no time to mope over Rob Pelton or feel sorry for myself. George dropped over Wednesday after dinner, but he didn't stay long. I got the feeling he was backing off from me, afraid that he had overstepped his territory the evening before. As he was leaving, I invited him back for supper the next night.

I had barely spoken two words to JoAnn since the weekend. Thursday morning the front office was busy because it was publication day. By the time I was ready to take my lunch, I found out JoAnn was already gone. I wondered what was going on with her lately. Then I remembered JoAnn mentioning there was a new man in her life—the doctor.

"Oh, did Mr. Pendergast tell you?" Marion said later that afternoon. "Sara's coming back. He thinks she'll be in next week."

"That's wonderful news."

"Maybe," said Marion. "Unless you have her job."

"No thanks."

"I'm only kidding. But really, Winnie, I read your article on the Peltons. It's so well done. You should do more of that kind of writing for the paper."

Before I could comment, the telephone rang and I answered it.

"Good afternoon. *Spundale Star.*"

"May I please speak to Mrs. Winnie Grant?" It was a woman.

"This is Mrs. Grant. What can I do for you?"

"Winnie, it's Irene Pelton. We haven't received our paper yet."

I settled back in my chair. "Well, it's only four o'clock, Mrs. Pelton. Maybe the delivery boy hasn't come around yet."

Irene sighed. "Possibly."

"I'll tell you what, though. Call me back later if it still hasn't been delivered and I'll see what I can do."

"Well, all right. I'm very eager to read your article."

After I hung up, I looked up the list of paperboys and ran my finger down it until I came to the name of Greg Peterson. He was Shirley's son, who had the paper route in the Pelton Drive area. I dialed the number next to his name. A child answered and told me Greg was not there. I knew Shirley was still at work, so I decided to call again later.

When I got home, I checked my mailbox and noticed JoAnn down the street, just pulling into her driveway. JoAnn saw me and walked over.

"Jo, where have you been this week?" I explained how I had been trying to see her.

"I went out with Martin again last night," she said, "and the night before." She sighed.

"Come on inside," I invited. "Sounds like you're getting along well with this guy." I unlocked the door and we entered. "I want to hear all the details."

"It goes both ways," JoAnn said. "First, tell me all about your dinner at Pelton Manor. Was Rob there?"

I poured two glasses of iced tea and joined JoAnn at the kitchen table. "No, he wasn't." I quickly went over what I knew.

"Oh." JoAnn removed her glasses and wiped them. "Well, I'll tell you, I've never met anyone like Martin. I feel we've known each other all our lives."

"And you just met him?" I teased. I wanted to ask how

serious this relationship was getting, but hesitated. I had the feeling there was something uncommon about JoAnn's newfound love.

"Well, it must be a relief for George, anyway," said JoAnn.

"What?"

"You know." JoAnn crinkled her nose. "Rob leaving Spundale. Winnie, George happens to care a lot about you, or haven't you noticed?"

"George is just a friend," I reaffirmed, "nothing more."

"Actually, I think George is a fantastic catch," JoAnn resumed. "I mean, he's handsome, intelligent, loyal. He reminds me of a big, lovable teddy bear sometimes."

I rolled my eyes. "A teddy bear, Jo?"

"If you're smart, Winnie, you'll grab him before someone else comes along. Guys like George Wyatt don't grow on trees, you know."

Before I could comment, the telephone rang. It was Irene Pelton again. She was convinced the paperboy had forgotten to deliver their paper, so I promised to get to the bottom of it.

JoAnn finished her tea and made an excuse to leave. "You and George behave yourselves tonight," she called as she slipped out the door.

I couldn't understand why JoAnn was so in favor of George. Didn't she recall how much I had suffered over losing Rob when we were teenagers? Maybe I was expecting JoAnn to react like she had ten years ago, the best friend whose shoulder was there for me to cry on. Well, not anymore, apparently. I almost wished I hadn't told her anything about meeting Rob again. "She probably thinks I'm acting very fickle and childish," I muttered to myself.

I got on the phone and called the Petersons. This time Shirley answered. "Oh yes, I remember now. Winnie Grant. We met last week at lunch."

I asked if Greg was back from delivering his route.

"He's out playing ball at the neighbors'," replied Shirley, "but he was done with his route earlier this afternoon. Why?

What's wrong?"

"Mrs. Pelton called me. It seems they didn't get their paper."

"Oh dear. That boy. I thought we had settled this ghost business once and for all, but I guess I was wrong."

I suggested coming over and driving Greg to Pelton Manor myself. Maybe I could convince Greg that it was safe.

"I hate to put you out," said Shirley, "but it's obvious the boy won't listen to his own mother."

After getting directions to the Petersons' house, I arrived there fifteen minutes later. They lived on one of the streets before the railroad tracks near Pelton Drive. I could smell a roast cooking when I entered the Petersons' spacious tri-level home. Greg sat on the sofa with a football helmet on his head. He looked up at me a second, then stared down at his feet.

Shirley crossed her arms. "Greg, Mrs. Grant is going to drive you over to the old manor."

Greg stood up and picked up an issue of the *Star* that was lying on the coffee table.

"Take your helmet off first," Shirley ordered.

Without a word, Greg removed his helmet and followed me outside to my car. He climbed into the passenger seat and I started up the engine. The sun was setting.

"I guess you like football," I said.

"Yes." He looked up at me. "You're not going to fire me, are you?"

I smiled. "No, Greg, I'm not going to fire you." I drove a ways, then said, "I just want to prove to you that there's nothing scary or evil about Pelton Manor."

"Have you been there?"

"Yes. A few times."

"And did you see any ghosts?"

"Of course not."

"Well, *I* did!" His eyes were round.

"Greg, when did you see a ghost?"

"One day when I was taking the paper up to the house, I

saw it," he told me. "It looked down at me from a window. I've seen it twice! It gave me the creeps both times."

"Which window?"

"I'll show you when we get there."

"What you probably saw, Greg, was a person. That's all. There aren't any ghosts at Pelton Manor."

"Oh yes, there is!" insisted Greg. "My friend Billy says that when someone dies in their own house, their ghost stays there and haunts it—and somebody died there last summer."

We were silent the rest of the way. Then I drove the Dodge into the driveway that led up to the old estate. A gust of wind blew a flock of brown leaves across the lawn in a whirling fashion. I noticed a strange car parked beside Rose's convertible and pulled up next to it.

Greg peered out the car window, his face pressed against the glass. "There! In that side window up there. That's where I saw the face!"

I leaned over to see at which window Greg was pointing. It was hard to see in the growing darkness, but he indicated one of the small third floor attic windows. I was reminded of my tour of the manor and Irene explaining that the third floor of the manor was not used.

"Well, you know what?" I told Greg. "That window does look spooky to me. But you know what else?"

"No."

"I've been in this old house—and I've even been upstairs in this old house—and I know that there aren't any ghosts up there."

He looked at me curiously. "You *know* these people?"

"That's right. Come on. Let's give them their paper." I started to get out of the car, but Greg stayed. "Well, come on."

Hesitantly, he opened the car door and stepped out. Then he walked with me up to the front door and I rang the bell. "Afraid?"

He looked up at me. "I don't think so."

The door opened and I let out a small gasp. I hadn't been

prepared for what was before me. Rob Pelton stood there, tall and handsome, a smile spread across his face as he recognized me. I was so startled, I couldn't speak.

"Well, hello," he said. Then he saw Greg. "And who is this?"

Irene came to the door just then. "Oh, come in," she called. "I see you've not only delivered the paper, but the paper*boy* as well."

My heart was beating wildly as Greg handed the newspaper to Mrs. Pelton, who thanked him. Greg gazed around at the decorated walls and paintings in the foyer. Rob stood in the same spot, gazing at me and smiling the whole time.

Irene put her arm around her son's back. "We didn't know Rob was coming back home. It was such a wonderful surprise." She looked down at Greg. "Young man, you will deliver the paper on time from now on, won't you?"

Greg nodded his head.

"I think..." I had to swallow before I could finish the sentence. "I think I've convinced him there are no ghosts." I rubbed Greg's head and hoped my hand wasn't trembling too violently. "You see, Greg? Only nice people live here."

Footsteps could be heard walking away. I caught a glimpse of Mrs. McCloskey going around the corner. Apparently she had been listening in.

"Can you stay awhile? Perhaps Mrs. McCloskey will fix our little man a nice glass of ginger ale."

"I'm afraid we can't stay," I protested. "Greg's mother has supper waiting for him."

As I turned to leave, I met the look in Rob's eye and something churned within my soul. I wasn't paying any attention to what Irene was saying. When we got to the car, I helped Greg get in, then glanced over my shoulder to see that Rob was still watching me.

15

A Proposal

AFTER I drove Greg home, I returned to my house and threw a couple of pork chops into a frying pan. Then I popped a couple of potatoes into the microwave. I had absolutely no appetite. I had come home in a daze. I kept remembering how Rob had watched me the entire time, but had barely said a word. I hadn't expected to see him again—*ever*. Why was he home at the manor? Would he leave again like before? Was there a chance I might run into him again?

As the clock approached seven, I made up my mind that I wasn't going to be moody. I forced myself out of the daze. I was steaming the broccoli spears when a knock came on the back door. I hurried to let George in.

"Mmm. Smells pretty good in here, Fred."

"It ought to," I said. "I hope you're starved."

George took off his jacket and fumbled around in one of its pockets. I took two plates from the cupboard and saw that he was still standing in the same spot. His hands were behind him and he smiled as if he knew something I did not.

"What's the matter, George?"

"Oh, nothing." He walked over to the table and set down a bottle of red wine. "I just thought this might come in handy tonight."

"George! You didn't have to do that!"

We sat down to a leisurely supper and George told me about

the day's events at the high school. His witty adventures never ceased to amuse me. This time I was careful not to drink a lot. The wine was very potent, however. By the time we finished eating, I felt better than I had all day. Thoughts of Rob Pelton were in the back of my mind.

George helped me gather up the dishes. "This is the way I like you to be," he said.

"What? Drunk?"

"You're not drunk."

"Well, okay. Tipsy." I giggled. The next thing I knew, George was running water in the sink. I told him to leave the dishes. I could take care of them later.

"Talkative," said George as he followed me into the living room. "I like you when you're talkative and cheerful." We sat down on the couch.

"Well, looks like you're going to have to bring a bottle of wine from now on."

"You only had a little bit," he scoffed.

"But a little bit is all I need." I suddenly realized that he was sitting on the sofa against me, his arm around me, and it felt very cozy.

"Say, that was a very tasty supper you fixed us," said George. His fingers stroked the side of my neck and it felt good just to rest there against his shoulder and listen to him talk. "Things like that are very important to us lonely bachelors."

"Really? Are you a lonely bachelor?" I just couldn't help how I felt, sort of giddy and loose.

"Well, let's hope not for long." He was serious when he said it. He looked into my face and smiled. Then, before I knew it, his mouth touched mine. I didn't resist. I even enjoyed kissing him. It was the first time George had ever kissed me. His warmth and tenderness gave me feelings inside that I hadn't felt in a long while.

A surge of desire suddenly rose within me so strong, my heart began to hammer. I opened my lips and welcomed his probing tongue. He fumbled to hold my relaxing body as we slid against the back of the sofa. Prickles of emotion I had long forgotten surfaced as my hungry mouth opened wider to draw him in. A moment later he released me and his blue eyes seemed to sparkle with surprise. "Wow," he murmured. "That was awesome. How do you feel?"

"Beautiful. I want to stay this way forever." I was hardly aware of what I was saying. The wine had taken over and I felt very mellow and rather sleepy.

"That's because you are." His fingers gently caressed my hair. "Beautiful, I mean." Again his mouth covered mine and we kissed longer this time. I had always assumed George's experience with women was limited because he had never made a pass at me before. But his gentle yet demanding caresses awakened a provocative cord within me I never knew I possessed. My mind went immediately to the question of "what next?" Would he undo my bra? And if he did, how could I resist when his kisses were this delicious?

"George..." I broke away. "Let me catch my breath..."

He drew me close beside him and held me. "Oh, I almost forgot." He reached into his pants pocket.

"What?"

"Just this." He produced a miniature black velvet box.

"What is it?" My eyes widened as I sat up, straight and alert.

"Here. You open it."

My fingers trembled as I took the box from him. I knew this was not something one of his friends had rejected and passed on to him. Before I opened the lid, I already knew what it contained. The rock sparkled as it caught the lamp light in half a dozen places. I could only sit and stare at it, unable to react.

George removed the ring from the box. "Do you like it?"

What could I say? I had never seen a more beautiful diamond ring. "Well, I... I... George, it's very pretty."

"Give me your hand."

"Wh-what?"

"Try it on." He grabbed my left wrist and was about to slip

the ring on my finger when he stopped. He had noticed the bands I still wore. "Oh, I didn't know you still wore..."

I withdrew my wrist from his. "I can't get them off," I confessed.

"You're kidding."

"No."

"What about soap and water?"

"I've tried that."

"Well..." George sighed. He looked so baffled, sitting there, holding a diamond engagement ring, and not sure what to do next.

"And haven't you forgotten something?" I said. "You didn't ask."

"Fred, I just assumed you felt the same way I do. I think we make a great team, you and I... There's no one else I'd rather spend my life with."

I began to protest, "Oh, George..." The telephone started ringing before I could say anything more. "Now who can that be? I hope it's not my boss. I'm in no condition to talk rationally." I reached over and picked up the receiver. "Hello."

"Hello, Winnie," said a man's voice.

"Who..." I stopped. It was Rob Pelton. I recognized his voice.

"It's Rob," he said.

"Oh." I hoped the vibrations from my pounding heart were not being transmitted over the wire.

"I read your article in the paper," he continued. "I enjoyed it immensely."

"You read it?" Foolish question.

"Yes."

George sighed impatiently beside me. "Well, it wasn't anything spectacular," I said. I began winding the telephone cord around my finger.

"I think it was." There was a pause, and then he said, "Rose and I talked tonight. I learned a few things I didn't know before."

"You... you did? What... what things did she tell you?"

He paused. "Things." Then he asked, "Winnie, I want to see you. Can I pick you up tomorrow night?"

I could hardly believe it was happening. I suddenly wished I was completely sober, and even more, I wished I was alone in the house. I was afraid George could hear every word being said.

"Well, what do you say?" asked Rob. "Is it a date?"

"When?" I asked.

"Oh, how about seven? I'll come by. Where do you live?"

"1406 Willow Street." After he said goodbye and I gently replaced the receiver in its cradle, I could still feel my heart pounding. I noticed my palms were sweating.

Suddenly, George grabbed me and began embracing me wildly. "You didn't forget about me, did you?" He laughed, then bent forward to kiss me.

I pulled away.

"Hey..." George's voice softened. "That wasn't bad news, was it?"

I wanted to say, "For you it is," but I faked a smile. "No, it wasn't bad news."

"Come here, then." He drew me close to him.

I then remembered the ring in his hand and my mouth opened to speak, but nothing came out.

"Fred, what is it? What's wrong?"

"George, please don't take this the wrong way. I..." The look in his eyes caused my face to collapse. I burst into tears and couldn't look at him. "Oh, my god..."

"Fred, what did I do? What did I say? I didn't mean to make you cry." He took hold of my hand and squeezed it. "Come on, snap out of it. Wipe those tears away. This is no way to treat the guy you're going to marry."

I sniffed hard and composed myself the best I could. "I never said I would," I pouted.

"What?"

There was a silence as I came to my senses. I reached for a tissue and blew my nose. George just sat there next to me, gazing down at the black velvet box. Slowly he put the ring back inside.

"Please don't misunderstand me, George." I smiled, but I knew it wasn't convincing. "I don't know what's got into me lately. I just didn't expect you to show up with an engagement ring."

"Don't apologize." George stood up and stuffed the box into his pocket. "It's my fault. Maybe I'm too impatient. It hasn't even been a year since you lost your husband."

"No, George, that's not it. You know that."

"I think I understand," he said. "I'll go now."

"You're leaving?" I stood up too.

"Get some rest, Fred." He found his jacket and put it on without a word. I felt I should say something in protest, but under the circumstances I really *did* want to be left alone just then. He looked at me and sort of smiled—more a smile of pity than of affection—then he walked out the door.

16

Love Requited

"HE'S BACK in town?" JoAnn tilted her glasses from across the restaurant table. "And you're going out with him *tonight?*" Her chin dropped in surprise.

We were having lunch the next day and I had just told JoAnn about Rob's telephone call. "Yes." I smiled, still overwhelmed by what had occurred.

"Oh Winnie, I can't believe it." For a second I thought JoAnn was disappointed in me. Then she sighed good-naturedly. "I was hoping you could come over and meet Martin tonight."

"I do want to meet him," I assured her, "but not tonight."

JoAnn lifted her coffee cup to her lips, but stopped before she drank. "Does George know yet?"

"No."

"Well, he's bound to find out sooner or later."

I spread my napkin over my lap. The sudden reminder of George conjured up the wild ecstasy I had felt last night when he had kissed me. I promptly stifled my emotions. "I'd rather not say anything to George until I have to." I almost related to JoAnn George's proposal last night, but for some reason I didn't want to make an issue out of it. George certainly didn't deserve being the subject of gossip, even between best friends.

I was glad when the day was over and I was able to go home and get ready for the evening. I hadn't been able to stop thinking about Rob all afternoon. As a result, my stomach hurt and I was a case of nerves. I had made several errors in some letters I had typed for Mr. Pendergast, which he brought to my attention.

The telephone rang just as I stepped out of the shower. I slipped into my bathrobe and wrapped a towel around my wet hair. My mother, calling from Arizona, said that they were planning to drive up for Thanksgiving and spend the week with me. Glancing at my calendar hanging next to the refrigerator, I saw that Thanksgiving was less than a week away. Where had the time gone?

We talked a while until I explained that I wasn't dressed and had to go. Then, while I was getting ready, George called.

"Listen, Fred, I've got a fantastic idea. How'd you like to go to a concert tonight?" he said. "The high school stage band is putting it on and I can get us in for free."

"Well, George, I..."

"Or if you don't like that, we can go see the new movie that's in town."

"George, I don't think so. Not tonight."

"Oh, well. That's that," he said before I could think of an excuse. "How was your day?"

"Fine," I said, "and yours?"

"So-so."

"George, I've got to go."

"Okay. Sure, Fred. See you later."

After I hung up, I stood there for a moment, thinking about George. I wondered if I should have said something then about having a date tonight with Rob Pelton. After all, I was sure George would understand. We had always been truthful with each other.

I was dressed and ready at ten minutes to seven. I puttered around nervously, straightening up so nothing looked out of place. When I heard a car in the driveway, I felt as if an electric current had passed through my body. Peeking out a corner of the window, I saw that it was Rob's car. Now if I could just remain calm. I had been unable to eat, so hadn't bothered to fix any supper. All of a sudden, I felt a hunger twinge.

I went to open the door. Rob stood there and smiled. His thick auburn hair had been combed back. A few strands blew over his forehead from the chilly breeze. For a moment I seemed to lose all control. The years had been long, even if we had already seen each other twice since ten years ago. I tried to find the right words to say, to invite him in, but our eyes had locked and I felt hypnotized.

Finally, I caught my breath and managed to invite him in.

"Rose says there's a new movie in town," said Rob. "I thought we could catch the late show."

"Then we have plenty of time," I said. "We could stay here a while... unless..."

"I'd like that." Rob followed me into the living room, where he sat down. I took a seat facing him. "I like your house," he said.

I felt uneasy. He was just trying to be polite. No place could compare to the elegance of Pelton Manor. My mind raced as I struggled to think of things to say. I couldn't help but notice that Rob seemed as nervous as I. "How long will you be in Spundale?" I asked.

"Actually, I'm here on a short leave of absence," he replied.

"For how long?"

"I don't know yet." After an embarrassing silence, he added, "I felt the need to get away for a while. From my work, that is."

I simply nodded. Then he began asking questions about me and my work. Before long we both were feeling a lot less uptight. I explained about my involvement with the local Audubon chapter.

Rob glanced at his watch and said, "If we're going to catch that show, we'd better leave now."

I put on my coat and turned out the lights. There was a cold wind from the north when we stepped outside. As we headed for his car, I tightened the coat around myself.

"If you recall, we saw many movies together," Rob remarked while he drove toward downtown.

I shivered. The car's heater was still blowing cold air. "I remember," I said through chattering teeth.

Rob fidgeted with some dials on the dash and then soft music filtered throughout the car. I leaned back and relaxed, recalling the summer nights we had spent as two kids draped in each other's arms at the outdoor theater, or holding hands at the Esquire with its air conditioning. And here I sat, freezing, next to a man who had become a stranger to me.

By the time the car had warmed up, we arrived downtown and had to face the cold again. We walked three blocks from the parking lot. The wind blew fiercely and Rob drew me close.

A group of high school kids loitered in front of the movie theater. They made me think of George. I wondered if any of them had Mr. Wyatt for their chemistry teacher. Rob squeezed my hand. He must have been remembering when the two of us had been that age.

After we were seated inside and the previews began, Rob found my hand and I thrilled at his touch. He smiled down at me and I returned his smile, dazzled by memories of his boyish face. I wanted to gaze at his face, but the feature was beginning. I was content just to sit close to him, the warmth of his fingers enfolding my own.

The film turned out to be a love story. At first I thought I was going to like it. The heroine was a young woman from the nineteenth century who married her childhood sweetheart. But suddenly the plot took a sour turn. The husband had a wandering eye and started favoring saloon girls. The innocent wife became a victim of her husband's infidelity, trapped in a one-sided marriage. I began to tense up in my seat.

Rob must have sensed the disturbance in me. He kept glancing at me. In the midst of an emotion-packed bedroom scene, I felt my hand sweating and withdrew it from Rob's. He leaned over and asked, "Do you want to leave?"

Suddenly I felt foolish. After all, this was some filmmaker's idea of art. It was probably a good story, but it was bringing forth some hidden pain from my recent past. I could identify too readily with the main character. I wanted to leave, but I didn't want to disappoint Rob. The least I could do was sit it out. "No," I whispered back, "it's okay."

But it wasn't okay. I was on the verge of tears and wondered if I should quick run to the restroom before my emotions overcame me.

Rob straightened in his seat and, before another minute had elapsed, took my hand forcefully and stood up. "Come on," he said.

I grabbed my purse and coat, and we got up and left the theater. I thought I had never felt more relieved to get out into the cold. Rob hadn't even bothered to try and get refunds on our tickets. If it had been George, it would have been very different, I was sure.

"We could have stayed," I told Rob as we strolled down the sidewalk.

"No, I didn't care for that film either," he said. "I wouldn't have taken you to that one except that nothing else is playing —except a Disney movie down the street."

I thought of something that made me smile. George had wanted to see the new movie that was in town. I could well imagine what would have happened. He would have taken me to see *Pinocchio* or *Peter Pan* instead.

"What are you smiling about?" pressed Rob.

"Nothing."

"The town certainly has changed in the time I've been away," he commented. I couldn't tell if he missed Spundale or was putting it down. We crossed the street and stepped into a small establishment with loud music playing and some freaky lights. The singer was a college girl with long blonde hair and a guitar. She had the microphone set too loud, so you couldn't hear your own voice.

"What?" I shouted to Rob after he had asked something.

"Hungry!" was all I heard.

I nodded my head. There was a break as the singer played a few stanzas between verses.

"How about a sandwich?"

"Fine."

"Wine or beer?" he asked.

I told him either was fine, so he ordered a couple of submarines and a small pitcher of wine that was on tap. Then we found a small table as far from the entertainment and the junior college crowd as possible. I had been hungry and the sandwich tasted great. The female vocalist quit playing and the place quieted down.

We talked about my job some more, which led to a discussion of the article I had written. Out of curiosity, I asked Rob if he had ever had access to the third floor at the manor.

"Oh sure," he said, "although nobody ever went up there much. There's the heating problem. Besides, two floors are already more than enough for my mother and sister-in-law."

I thought about it while sipping my wine.

"You look puzzled," said Rob.

I wanted to mention how I had asked to see the third floor during my tour of Pelton Manor, and how Irene had denied me the opportunity. But I didn't.

"I'm sorry about what happened to your husband," said Rob.

"You wouldn't remember Alan."

"No, I don't recall him at all." Rob reached across the table and touched my hand. "I know it had to be hard on you. I feel so badly that I only found out about it last night."

I looked into those compassionate brown eyes and all of a sudden found myself spilling all the details of Alan's death. He listened carefully to each word until I had finished, then poured another glass of wine for each of us.

"I'm sorry about your brother and your father," I told him, then added, "I remember your dad very well, but I never got the chance to meet Benjamin."

Rob stared into his glass. "The accident was a terrible thing."

"So, you do believe it was an accident," I commented.

Rob glanced at me, startled. "It never occurred to me to be anything else. Why do you ask?"

I explained how I had been to see the old aunts and had listened to their theory.

Rob made a face. "Don't believe anything those old ladies tell you," he said. "Naturally, the incident was investigated. The coroner's verdict was satisfactory to everyone."

"And what about your father?" I asked. "What caused his death?"

"He died because of that stroke."

I wondered if I should tell him that Rose had other ideas regarding their father's death. As I lifted the glass to my lips, I caught sight of a man across the room watching me. He was a heavyset man in his mid-forties, with a ruddy complexion and bristly beard. He looked familiar to me. He wore an open sheepskin coat over a plaid shirt. When he noticed my stare, he slowly averted his eyes and drank some beer.

"Looks like the break is over," mentioned Rob.

"What?" I turned my attention back to him. Then I saw the blonde-haired singer carry her guitar back toward the microphone. She proceeded to warm up for her next set.

Rob finished the rest of his wine. "Want to leave?"

"Sure." Again I noticed the bearded man across the room, but couldn't place him. Getting up from the table, I felt slightly dizzy from the wine. I told Rob I had to visit the ladies' room.

When I came out, I didn't see him anywhere. Putting on my coat, I started out the door. I saw Rob, whose back was toward me, speaking to that same man who had been watching me inside the bar. The bearded man turned sharply and disappeared around the corner.

"There you are," I said.

Rob grinned and reached his arm out to me. "Let's go."

"Where?"

"Trust me." We walked toward the parking lot.

"Rob, who was that man you were just talking to?"

He was silent for a moment, then said, "Nobody. He wanted

directions."

I told him how I had noticed the man watching me in the bar. "And I can't get it out of my head that I've seen him somewhere before."

"Oh?" He tightened his grip around my waist and I leaned against him, welcoming the warmth and the closeness of his presence. "Are you sure you don't want to see the end of the movie?"

I laughed. "Do you?"

Rob laughed softly. "I've got something better in mind." It sent a thrill of anticipation through me.

He drove out past the manor. "Remember this road?" he asked as we turned onto a private back road that led into the woods.

"Yes." I would never forget this bumpy road. It took us into a secluded spot where we used to come to park.

When we approached the end of the drive, Rob stopped the car. "What's this?" he asked.

I saw what he meant. Half a dozen other cars were parked along the side. Suddenly, heads popped up in every one, disturbed by our headlights. The next minute I burst out giggling. "Our spot has been discovered."

Rob sighed, then turned to me and smiled. "Nothing is sacred anymore." Then he shifted into reverse and backed up all the way down the road.

We returned to my house, where I fixed some coffee.

"I drink it black," Rob called into the kitchen.

I brought a tray of cups and the coffee pot into the living room and set them on the coffee table. "Well, I must admit, you have changed," I told him, remembering the seventeen-year-old boy who had managed to swallow a cup of coffee only after diluting it with cream and five tablespoons of sugar.

"And you have changed," he said.

I sat down on the couch next to him and poured the coffee.

"Oh, have I?" I caught him staring and blushed. "I was afraid we'd get into the wrong light and you'd see that wrinkle."

He didn't say anything right away and I felt strangely shy.

"You're still the Winnie Remington I remember," he said after a minute, "but your hair is different, and you've grown a smidgen more beautiful. If anything, you've changed for the better."

I sipped some coffee, but it was too hot and burned my tongue. I felt a sudden strangeness come between us in the silence that followed. He drank his coffee and I recalled the years that had passed—all the empty months after Rob had gone off to college. I wanted to ask him why. Why had he never telephoned or written to me? Why had he caused all the tears, anguish and misery in my adolescent life?

Rob set his cup down and reached for my hand. "Winnie, there's something I... I don't know quite how to say it." His hand felt warm and good in mine as he began stroking my fingers one by one.

I could feel ripples of excitement flowing. He hung his head. "I doubt if you'll ever know how sorry I am. It was wrong of me never to call you or answer any of your letters."

I felt overcome by the sound of his voice. I wanted to fall into his arms right then and forgive him without hearing his explanation, but something held me back.

"I wanted to," he said. "I missed you."

"But you had your studies," I said. "I understand that now. I knew how important school was for you."

"No, it was wrong of me," he continued. I didn't want to hear the rest. Any moment now he would confess how he had fallen in love with a co-ed. It was inevitable. Rob rubbed my hand and gazed into my eyes. "Nothing was ever *that* important. I admit, I thought it was important at the time. I look back on it now and I realize how immature I was." He shook his head.

Rob, please don't say it, my mind pleaded.

"Then when I thought I'd try to see you again," he resumed, "it was too late. I remember exactly how it was. I had come home for winter break between semesters. I was reading the newspaper the first morning I was home and I happened to see the engagement announcement of a certain Winnie Remington —to some guy I had never heard of before."

I could feel my eyes blur as he continued.

"And you may not believe this, but I was hurt. It shocked me, in fact. Ruined my two weeks of vacation. Because, I'm telling you, Winnie, I've never stopped thinking about you. Never in these past several years."

I trembled through the next few moments. The words I had so long awaited, the words that dissolved the fears, that lifted the agony from all the years of despair, had finally reached my ears. I couldn't have fantasized a more satisfying answer to that plaguing question, why.

"Do you forgive me?" His voice was soft and pleading. In that moment I saw everything I had ever wanted in Rob's eyes.

"Forgive you?" I was so choked with emotion, I could hardly get the words out. "Oh Rob... yes." I fell into his arms as he gathered me up. I could feel the pounding of his heart. Then he kissed me, long and hard, and it felt so good to be just where I had wanted to be for so long.

I could feel the strong wave of magic that swept over me. I was unable to resist it. Rob's mouth was firm, yet tender, as his lips explored my face, neck and shoulders, sending thrilling sensations to every nerve in my body. He laid me down on the couch and his feverish lips found my left ear lobe, sending ripples of pleasure throughout me. Next I felt his hand exploring my breasts. His hand cupped a breast and his fingers gently kneaded it. Surges of excitement shot through me and I arched my neck as he kissed my ear.

"I love you," he murmured. "Winnie, I've always loved you."

His touch sent shivers up and down my body.

"Rob..." I was so ready for him, my head swam. I wanted him to remove my dress. I clung tightly to him. I felt I could never love someone more than I did just then. I wanted to become totally possessed by Rob. I had fantasized it time after time in the long years we had been separated, but suddenly it was as if we had never been apart.

The evening might have ended differently had the phone not interrupted us. I was tempted not to answer it, but the mood was broken as Rob lifted himself up. I answered the telephone on the fifth ring. It was Rob's mother, Irene. She asked to speak to him.

"Sure, Rob's right here." I handed the receiver to him, then caught my breath. Finally, I got up to clear the coffee cups.

From the kitchen I heard him speak in short phrases to his mother, and then he hung up.

"Everything all right?" I asked.

"Yup." He picked up his jacket. "I'm sorry, Winnie, but I have to go."

"Oh... why?"

He gathered me into his arms once again. "It's nothing you need to worry about." He kissed me fervently and it sent waves of passion flowing once again. Then he pulled away.

"What did your mother want?" I asked.

"You are so beautiful..."

"Rob, aren't you going to answer me?"

"It's nothing, I promise you." He stroked my cheek and smiled. Then he kissed me again, deeper. Moments later I had forgotten my concern over the phone call. At the time I truly believed nothing could spoil our happiness or the unspoken promise of our future together.

17

Lunch at the Manor

WHEN I awoke Saturday morning, I knew I wasn't the same woman I had been the day before. The memory of last night with Rob and the rekindling of our love filled me with a euphoria I could not shake. My dreams had been full of Rob and the warmth of his kisses. At least I *thought* it was Rob in my dreams. Who else could it have been? I didn't want to ruin it all by remembering too much.

Rob telephoned and invited me over to the manor for lunch. I could not wait to see him again. For some reason every moment seemed precious. We had so much time to make up.

As my car approached the Victorian estate, I noticed how much more forlorn the place looked now. Barely a leaf was left on the grotesque branches of the willows that draped the old house. I pulled up into the driveway and parked. Rob had seen me and came out of the house to meet me. I smiled up at him and he immediately took me into his arms. Our mouths touched and the desire flooded through me as he drew me closer and prolonged the kiss.

"Are you two going to stand out there all day?" called a voice.

I pulled away and saw Rose standing on the porch. Rob's sister tossed her long dark hair and grinned at us. As we approached, locked in each other's arms, I could see the delight in Rose's eyes. She didn't have to say anything. It was written all over her face that she was glad we were back together.

We stepped inside the manor. As we passed the hallway on our way into the living room, Mrs. McCloskey's voice rang out from the kitchen and Irene's rose above it.

"What are Mother and Mrs. McCloskey arguing about?" Rob asked Rose, who had followed us in.

Rose shrugged. "I don't know." She lit a cigarette. "Say, listen. After lunch I'm driving to Lansing with some friends. Would you two like to come along?"

I glanced at Rob and saw that he had no interest in going. I smiled in relief. "Maybe another time."

Before Rose could comment, Marcia walked into the room, dressed in white slacks and a shimmery, low-cut blouse. Her eyes briefly encountered mine. There was a hint of indifference in her gaze, until her eyes fell on Rob. Suddenly, her whole disposition changed. She was no longer a cat lurking in the shadows, but a hungry lioness who had found some prey. Marcia's lips drew back and relaxed into a smile that was probably appealing, but at that moment filled me with sickening dread. With a slight sweep of her hand over her blonde hair, Marcia strolled to the couch and sat down, crossing her legs.

Rapid footsteps in the hall approached, and then Irene Pelton entered. "Oh, Winnie dear, I'm so glad you could make it." She beckoned to Rob and me to sit. "I don't think I got a chance to tell you how much we all enjoyed reading your article."

"Thank you."

"What's the matter with Mrs. McCloskey, Mother?" asked Rose. "It sounded like she was really upset about something this morning."

Irene seated herself and sighed. "Just the usual."

"I think the woman should have a vacation," said Marcia.

"Nonsense. She's only been with us a few weeks," protested Irene.

"I tried talking with her earlier," said Rose, "but she was really upset about something and I couldn't figure out what it was."

"It was just a bad dream she had," said Irene.

"You mean she's all upset over a silly dream?" Marcia scoffed.

"That's all it was, I'm sure." Irene frowned. "Rose, I wish you'd stop smoking. You know how I feel about your smoking."

Irene turned to me. "You don't smoke, do you, Winnie?"

"No," I said quietly.

"But Marcia smokes," argued Rose. "Her smoking never seems to bother you."

"Marcia is not my daughter." Irene sighed and looked at me. "What does a mother do with a daughter like Rose?"

"Excuse me." Rose left, obviously offended.

"It's just that Rose has always been such an impulsive, uncontrollable child," Irene continued, not paying any attention to the fact that Rose had left the room. "She's such a tramp. Otto and I could never keep her restrained. That's why we felt it to be of no use to argue when she went off on that motorcycle trip last spring."

Rob cleared his throat. "Mother..."

"Then there was the time when Rose was in high school," Irene went on. "How old was she? Fourteen? Fifteen?"

"Mother," Rob repeated, "I think we should change the subject."

I waited to see what would happen next. I felt uncomfortable listening to Rose's mother expose all her faults. I had always been fond of Rose.

To everyone's relief, Marcia broke the tension by standing up and sighing in a bored fashion. "I think I'll go see if Mrs. McCloskey has lunch ready yet."

"Well." Irene looked at me, then Rob. "I imagine you young people would prefer to be alone."

I started to protest, but Rob took my hand and began caressing it. "Winnie is a bird freak," he told his mother. "I think she'd enjoy seeing the sanctuary you set up in the backyard."

"Oh yes," said Irene. "Why don't you two go out on the back patio? It's drafty out there, but the sun is shining today. I can have Mrs. McCloskey call you when lunch is served."

"That sounds like a good idea," said Rob. He led me through the hallway to the rear of the manor. When we passed the kitchen, Mrs. McCloskey stared out at us curiously.

"Where did Rose go?" I asked when we were out in the brisk air.

"Probably up in her room." Rob put his arm around me and nuzzled my head with his chin.

"I wonder if she's all right."

"Rose is a big girl."

"I know." But I was still bothered. I was sure that Rose, who was a grown woman, was embarrassed to have her mother criticize her in front of a guest.

The bird sanctuary was hardly Rob's true reason for getting me out of the house. He smiled down at me. "Do you feel it?"

"What?" But I already knew. The answer came as he smothered me in a passionate embrace. I immediately responded and after a few minutes had to tear away and catch my breath.

"They'll be coming for us any minute." I laughed.

"Do you know how lovely you are?" he told me. "Do you know how many nights I used to lay awake, just remembering your face and the sound of your voice?"

I felt so happy then. I felt my dreams were coming true.

"Lunch, Mr. Robert," Mrs. McCloskey called out the patio door. She disappeared before he could reply.

"Let's skip lunch and just have the dessert," he said.

I laughed. "Come on. The others are waiting."

Rose joined us after Rob and I were seated across from Irene and Marcia. Rose took her place at the table without a word to anyone. She ate her meal in silence, then got up and left to meet her friends who were going to Lansing. I wanted to talk with her, but decided later might be a better time.

"How'd you like to take a walk through the woods this afternoon?" suggested Rob after lunch. "Maybe we can go back and have a look at the old mill. Who knows, we might flush a few more pheasants."

I laughed. "Too bad I didn't think to bring my binoculars. It sounds wonderful." From across the table, I caught the grudge in Marcia's eyes.

Mrs. McCloskey stepped through the doorway to the dining room. "Excuse me, Mrs. Pelton, but Miss Pearl is on the phone. She sounds rather upset."

Irene got up from the table and followed the housekeeper out of the room.

"Isn't it rather cool out for a walk?" remarked Marcia.

"Not at all," said Rob.

"If I were Winnie, I wouldn't want to ruin a nice outfit like that." Marcia smiled her cat smile.

"This?" I glanced down at my slacks outfit.

"Winnie happens to be an outdoorswoman at heart," said Rob.

"I grew up with two older brothers. I couldn't help it, actually."

"Why don't you come with us?" Rob asked his sister-in-law. "The walk might do you some good."

"If you don't mind, I prefer to stay here," she replied, turning away.

"Rob," called Irene from the hall, "were you planning anything this afternoon?"

"What's up?"

Irene stepped into the dining room. "Aunt Pearl and Aunt Ophelia are having difficulties with their plumbing again. They need someone to come out and help them."

"Call the plumber," said Marcia. "Rob and Winnie were planning a hike."

Irene looked puzzled. "A what?"

"No, Mother." Rob sighed as he put down his napkin. "Tell them I'll be right over to have a look." He turned to me as Irene quickly left the room. "I don't know what I can do. It's probably nothing. You don't mind waiting here a little while, do you?"

"No, of course not."

Rob stood up. "I won't be gone too long."

Once Rob had left the room, I felt awkwardly alone with

Marcia. She didn't object when I got up and started clearing dishes. I carried them into the kitchen to Mrs. McCloskey. When I came out for another arm load, Marcia had left.

"Dear, you needn't do that," chided the housekeeper when I had returned to the kitchen with the last of the lunch dishes. "You're a guest here. What would Mrs. Irene say?"

"Oh, I don't mind," I said. "It will help to pass the time while Rob's over at the aunts' cottage. Besides, I did want to talk with you."

Mrs. McCloskey filled the sink with hot water. "Oh? I can't imagine what you want to talk to me about." I noticed as the housekeeper poured some detergent that her hand was shaking.

"How long have you worked for the Peltons, Mrs. McCloskey?"

"Let me see now. Since the middle of October. The fifteenth, to be exact. It's been too long, as far as I'm concerned."

"Don't you like it here? I think it's a fantastic place, especially for its age." I saw a dish towel over the back of a chair and reached for it.

"Too many things are going on in this house," she disclosed.

"What do you mean?"

Mrs. McCloskey hesitated. I could tell she was reluctant to say anything by the way she clattered the dishes in the sink and didn't look up.

"I won't repeat anything," I assured her. "What do you mean by *things going on in this house?*"

"Oh... noises, for one thing," she said.

"Noises?"

"Yes'm. I often hear strange noises, sometimes in the night, but especially when no one else is in the house."

"What kind of noises do you hear?"

"Unnatural ones. Sometimes bumps and scrapes. I really don't know how to explain it." She turned off the tap and began scrubbing a serving bowl. "And this house has got cold spots in it."

I stared at her, uncertain about what she meant.

"Sometimes I go into a room," she explained, "and a terrible chill will hit me. That's when I know I'm not alone in this house." She shook her head. "I should have listened to my sister-in-law and never taken this job. She worked here for quite a while, before the family tragedy. She moved in to work full-time afterwards, but moved out right away."

Mrs. McCloskey stopped washing dishes for a second and turned to look at me. "It's not that I mind working here, Mrs. Grant. I'm quite fond of Miss Rosie, and I get along with Mrs. Irene. I have even come to tolerate her headstrong daughter-in-law. It's this house I can't stand! Not after I saw what I did at the top of the stairs."

"Yes, Rose told me you had an experience. She said you thought you saw a man at the top of the stairs."

The housekeeper resumed her work as she spoke. "Miss Rosie's a sweet girl. It's a shame her mother's always picking on her. Yes, it happened two weeks ago, while I was going up to make the beds. Both Irene and Marcia had gone out shopping and Rosie was away that weekend. Suddenly he was there, staring right down at me."

"Can you describe what the man looked like?"

"Well, yes. He was young, about thirty, and had brown hair and a mustache. He was dressed in a robe of some sort—perhaps a lounging jacket or a bathrobe. He just stared down at me and, before I could catch my breath, he dematerialized."

I found her story pretty fantastic. "Did you tell Mrs. Pelton about it when she got home?"

"Of course I did. I was sitting in the parlor, still holding the linens when she came through the door and found me. I had been too scared to go anywhere else. Naturally, she didn't believe a word. But I'll tell you something else, Mrs. Grant. That was no *mortal* man looking down at me. I am quite certain that I saw Benjamin Pelton's ghost!"

"You're sure it was a real *ghost* you saw?"

"Very sure. You see, Mrs. Grant, I'm what is called a

sensitive."

"You've had previous psychic experiences?" I asked.

"Oh yes," the housekeeper replied. "When I was ten years old, I witnessed the death of my brother at the foot of my bed one morning, and three days later we received word of his death from overseas. I've had other such visions since then." She rinsed the bowl and handed it to me for drying. "That's why being in this house bothers me so much. There are so many things that aren't right. All the time I can feel a presence."

I dried the bowl and set it on the counter. "I have just one more question," I said. "Have you ever been up to the third floor?"

Footsteps echoed in the hall. A moment later, Irene stood in the doorway to the kitchen. "Winnie! Whatever do you think you are doing?"

"I was just giving Mrs. McCloskey a hand with these lunch dishes," I replied.

Irene looked perturbed. "I can't allow you to do housework when you're a guest at the manor. Now, put down that dish towel and come out of there!" Irene glared at the housekeeper. "Certainly you should know better than to take advantage of our guest. Come along, Winnie."

I felt like a juvenile delinquent as I dropped the towel over the back of a chair and followed her. I spent the good part of the afternoon sitting in the living room and conversing with Irene. Marcia was snuggled into one of the big cushioned chairs, reading a paperback. When it got to be four o'clock and Rob still had not returned from the aunts', I decided it was time to leave. I still had some grocery shopping to do.

"I'm sorry Rob was detained," apologized Irene, "but I'll tell him. I'm sure he'll understand."

"Tell Mrs. McCloskey it was a delicious lunch, and thank you for inviting me again." I turned to say goodbye to Marcia, but the other woman had her nose buried in her book.

18

Disappointment

THE AIR felt much cooler as I made my way to the car. The sunshine that had been out that morning had disappeared and the sky was gray with thick cloud cover. It had been just a week ago, I thought, climbing into the driver's seat, that I had come to the manor for my interview, unaware that in the brief days to follow I would find myself reunited with Rob Pelton.

When I drove to the end of the driveway, I turned my car toward the lane that led to the aunts' cottage. I wanted to explain to Rob why I was leaving. We would have our walk in the woods another day, before the snow came.

"Why, it's Mrs. Grant," Pearl called out the cottage door after I parked and got out. The terrier was barking fiercely from the vine-covered porch.

Ophelia stepped out the door and snatched the dog's collar. "Won't you come in?" Pearl smiled and wiped her hands on her apron.

"It's too bad you didn't come an hour ago," said Ophelia. "Rob was here."

"Yes, our nephew is home," said Pearl.

I stopped, puzzled. "You mean Rob's not here now?"

The sisters looked at one another, then back at me. "He was here earlier," explained Pearl. "We had a water problem."

"Our bathroom faucet was dripping," said Ophelia. "It was keeping us up at night."

"We telephoned and Irene sent Rob over to fix it," continued Pearl. "He is so handy, you know."

"And he left?" I stared blankly. "An hour ago?"

Both old ladies nodded vigorously. "Well, let's not stand out here gabbing," chided Ophelia. "Come inside. We have some fruit cake we want you to try."

I thanked the sisters but explained I was on my way home and couldn't accept their kind invitation today. After I left, I wondered what had happened to Rob. Where was he? If he had left the aunts' cottage an hour ago, why hadn't he returned to the manor? The cottage was only a few minutes away. He might have at least let me know if he had somewhere else to go. I rationalized that there most likely was a good explanation, and drove toward home.

On the way, I thought more about what Mrs. McCloskey had told me. I didn't know whether to believe what she said about seeing a ghost or not. I had always kept an open mind concerning psychic phenomena, although I had never had any experiences of my own.

Yet, Mrs. McCloskey claimed she had seen Benjamin in that house—Benjamin, who had met a tragic death. Was it possible? And what could she have told me about the third floor before Irene had interrupted us? What secrets, if any, were up there? Was the reason Irene didn't allow anyone to go up more than just a matter of safety?

The phone was ringing when I arrived home after grocery shopping, but it stopped before I could get to it. I thought to give JoAnn a ring, so after putting all the groceries away, I called her number. It was busy then, and when I tried a little later, there was no answer.

Rob came over a little later. I was happy to see him.

"I'm really sorry about this afternoon," he told me. "I had no idea their faucets were in such need of repair."

"No need to apologize." I felt secure in his embrace. I wanted to ask him where he had gone after he left the aunts' cottage. I didn't get a chance.

"Winnie." Rob held me back and looked at me seriously. "I have to leave for a while. I hate having to tell you this, but I have to leave Spundale this evening. I'm catching a plane in an hour."

I let out a sigh. "Why? Where are you going?"

"A small emergency back in Connecticut. The university needs me to fill in for a couple of days. Anyway, I'm hoping it's just for a couple of days."

"Oh no..."

He held me close again. "I hate to be away from you."

"I don't want you to go," I murmured.

"I know," he sighed, "but until I can find something else, I feel I should hang onto my position."

"Of course," I muttered. "But when will you come back?"

"I'll see what I can do once I get there." He stroked my hair. "Right now I can't make any promises."

I was too crushed to say anything. After a minute, Rob sighed and gently tilted my chin toward his face. "Hey, cheer up. It's not so bad. We've still got the rest of our lives ahead of us."

We kissed, but my heart felt heavy. I had a childish fear that after tonight another ten years might pass before we would meet again—only the next time I saw him, things would never be the same.

19

Rose's Dreams

REALITY CREPT back into my life Sunday. Rob's departure the night before had been hard on me. I knew he meant it when he said he hated to go, yet I had noticed a sense of urgency in him that disturbed me. When I had asked him what was bothering him, he had kissed me and told me there was nothing to worry about.

I didn't want to think about how long Rob might be gone. I was glad to have my parents' visit to look forward to with Rob away. I was cleaning the house that afternoon when Irene Pelton telephoned. The older woman sounded upset. "Winnie, I just don't know what to do. It's my housekeeper, Mrs. McCloskey. She's left."

"You mean, she quit?"

Irene explained that Mrs. McCloskey had packed up her things and left that morning. "I don't understand why she would do such a thing," said Irene. "I really thought she was getting along better and would stay on."

"Mrs. Pelton, were you aware of how afraid she was to stay in the manor?" I asked. "I'm sure it had nothing to do with you or Rose or Marcia."

"But that's silly," said Irene. "What is there to be afraid of? Her imagination? Who am I going to find to take her place? Well, listen dear, the reason I called you was to ask if you would help me find a replacement."

I hesitated before responding. It seemed odd to me that Mrs. Pelton needed somebody else to find her a housekeeper. But I couldn't say no to her—not to Rob's mother. "Of course, I'll help you find somebody," I finally said, "but I don't think we'll have much luck on a Sunday." I then suggested placing an ad in the *Spundale Star*.

"Oh dear, I don't think I can wait," fretted Irene. "Things are soon to be in such turmoil here."

It took some convincing before Irene finally admitted that hiring a new servant would have to wait until Monday. "I trust you, Winnie," she said. "Perhaps we can manage for another day." Then she sighed. "And maybe it was best that Mrs. McCloskey did leave."

"How do you mean?"

Irene began to stammer. "Oh well... I mean, like you said yourself, she was afraid to stay in this big house. And besides, her dreams kept interfering with her work. As a matter of fact, they were even getting on *my* nerves."

I spent the rest of the day preparing the extra bedroom for my parents to use. It was nearly nine o'clock when the doorbell rang. I answered it and found Rose Pelton standing there. "I know this is a bad time," said Rose. "I'm sorry to barge in on you like this, Winnie."

"It's no problem," I said and invited her in. "I'm always happy to see you. And I didn't get a chance to talk with you yesterday at the manor."

Rose sat down. "You must miss Rob now that he's gone."

"How did you guess?"

"Winnie, you have that look of love. I envy you." She crossed her legs and gazed around at the humble furnishings. "You have a nice place."

"Thanks. Sometimes I think it's too big for one person."

Rose opened a pack of cigarettes. "How would you like living at the manor?" She caught my expression and waved a finger. "Never mind. You'd probably love living in the manor. But remember, I've lived there all my life practically." She lit a cigarette. "Are you sure I'm not barging in?"

"Positive." I offered her a drink, but Rose declined. "Rose, is something wrong?"

Rose was not one to beat around the bush. She settled back in her chair. "Winnie, I just know there's something peculiar about Benjamin's death." She stared into space, then said, "I think somebody murdered him."

I blinked. "What makes you think that?"

"I'm not sure."

"Well, who do you suspect did it? Certainly you don't think your mother or Marcia..."

Rose looked at me in despair. "Winnie, I just can't bring myself to believe it was, but I keep having this awful feeling about it. I can't talk to my mother or Marcia about it because they always start crying when the subject comes up. It almost seems phony. I mean, I grieved over my brother. I loved him, too. But over time it wore off. I mean, it's been six months now."

"Are you saying you believe either Marcia or your mother are to blame?"

"No, but I believe they're not telling the truth about what happened that night." She sighed. "For one thing, their stories agree—as far as what went on in the house that night. You see, my mother and Marcia never used to agree on anything. They were always contradicting each other, always accusing each other of one thing or another. Now the two of them are pretty thick."

"Okay, Rose, but what actually makes you think your brother was murdered?"

"You're going to think this is silly."

"No, I won't."

She merely shook her head.

"What? Tell me," I begged.

"All right, but I know you're going to think it's ridiculous." She leaned forward. "I keep dreaming about it."

I prompted her to go on.

Rose tapped the end of her cigarette on an ash tray. "I have dreams about Ben. Practically every night. Sometimes they keep me awake because I'm afraid that when I go back to sleep, I'll keep dreaming about him."

"Tell me about them," I urged.

Rose took a puff and let it out. "Well, Ben calls to me. I'll be dreaming that I'm at a friend's house, or at a party, or anywhere, and all of a sudden I'll hear his voice calling out to me from the distance. *Ro-osie! Ro-osie!* It fades in and out of what goes on in the dream. Isn't that stupid?"

I assured her that it was not and she continued. "Sometimes in the dream I call back to him, but I can't make my voice work. Have you ever had dreams like that, when you try like hell to yell out and as hard as you try, you can't?"

I nodded.

"Well, it keeps on like that. Then, suddenly I'll dream I'm back home, sometimes in bed, and then I'll *see* Ben. All of a sudden he's standing there in front of me, staring right at me. He looks as if he never died, never left us—and he reaches out to me, trying to say my name, but I can't hear him anymore. And then, all of a sudden, I wake up." Rose's brown eyes began to well up. "Winnie, it's terrible to wake up and think he's still standing there in the dark. I get so frightened."

"How long have you had these dreams?" I asked.

"Gosh, I don't know. For months, I guess. I think they started last summer, after my dad died, but they quit when I lived away from home. Since I've been back, I've been having them again."

I thought Rose's dreams were very strange, but didn't see why she suspected somebody had murdered Benjamin. "What do you think the dreams mean?"

Rose shrugged. "I just get the feeling something's wrong. I feel like in the dreams Benjamin is trying to reach out to me, trying to get me to find out the truth."

I told Rose about the conversation I'd had yesterday with Mrs. McCloskey. "She told me about that man she saw at the top of the stairs."

"Did she tell you it was Ben she saw?" asked Rose.

"Yes, but I don't think she ever knew him, did she?"

"No. She might have seen pictures of him, though. Anyway, I was very upset when I learned Mrs. McCloskey had left this morning. I wish we could get her to come back." Rose took another puff and sank back into the armchair. "Poor Mrs. Mac."

We were silent for a minute. I recalled more of the things the housekeeper had revealed to me the day before. "Rose, do you ever hear noises in the manor?"

"Like what?"

"Mrs. McCloskey mentioned that she often heard scraping noises and bumps. I don't know if it was her imagination, or if you heard them too."

"You've got to remember," said Rose, "I've lived in the manor all my life and I'm used to every sound. And there are always noises in the night—the house settling, whatever. If there were any new noises, I think I'd have heard them too."

"What about cold spots?" I asked.

Rose's smile faded. "How do you mean?"

"Do you ever go into a room and suddenly feel chilled?" I told Rose about an article I had once read that said poltergeists liked cold temperatures, and how Mrs. McCloskey had claimed there were cold spots in Pelton Manor. "You're supposed to be able to tell if one is in the same room as you, if you feel a cold spot," I added.

"I didn't know that." Rose looked puzzled. "In fact, now that you mention it, there have been times when I've been sitting alone in the library or watching TV or something and I'll feel a draft. Only, I can't figure out where it's coming from. I'll be shivering with goose bumps on my arms and then my mother or Marcia will walk into the room and suddenly the cold is gone." She sighed. "Well, I've got to move out of the manor, Winnie. I've had just about all I can take from my mother nagging me."

"When are you planning to move out?"

"Soon."

"Where will you go?"

"I haven't really decided yet. I wish there was some way I could find out the truth about Ben before I go."

"I don't suppose you've come right out and asked your mother or Marcia," I said.

"They both still insist he fell down the stairs by accident and that they got up when they heard him fall. But, Winnie, I wonder sometimes... if my father were alive... what story he'd have to tell."

She took one more draw from her cigarette, then rubbed it out in the ash tray. "It puzzles me," she continued. "My father's death is more of a mystery to me than Ben's. Dying so suddenly when we were so sure he was getting better at Spider Lake. And then to have the services rushed through like they were. It was for my mother's sake, of course—a closed casket."

I remembered the obituary then and how it had seemed strange to me that friends had been asked to call at the manor instead of a funeral parlor. "Well, I suppose there are more and more funerals like that nowadays," I commented.

"Still," said Rose, "it bothers me about him." She sighed. "I'm glad I came over. I got a lot off my chest."

"Rose..." I began fidgeting, not sure if I should ask the next question. "The other night... when your mother called here... do you know what that was about?"

Rose shook her head. "No." I could tell she had not known about her mother's call. I decided not to press her with any more questions. What business was it of mine, after all, if Rob had been expecting an important call and had to leave? I offered to fix some tea and started toward the kitchen.

Rose got up and followed me. "I don't want to keep you up. I know you have to go to work in the morning."

"Nonsense." I filled the tea kettle with water and set it on the burner. "But to tell the truth, I'm really in no hurry to go to bed after talking about your dreams."

Rose laughed. Half an hour later, we felt more relaxed, chatting of less morbid matters, and Rose left in a cheerier mood than when she had come. I felt uneasy being alone in the house again, especially remembering the eerie dreams Rose was having of her dead brother.

I already knew Benjamin had been the favorite son. I remembered Rob saying to me once, "My brother Benjamin is my mother's greatest achievement. To her, he's the brightest, handsomest, most talented son anyone could have. I'd be lying if I said I wasn't jealous sometimes. But I never hated him for it." I got the feeling that Rob may even have felt sorry for his older brother who had been constantly under the stress of living up to the expectations of their domineering mother.

20

Marcia Sees All

JOANN AND and I had made plans the next day to have lunch. We had a lot to catch up on. But I was behind in my duties and had to cancel my lunch with her. When I stopped in at Advertising on my way home, JoAnn was out.

I would have walked over to my friend's house, but as I pulled into my driveway I noticed the fifth-wheel camper parked there. A light on in my kitchen meant that my parents had arrived.

My mother stepped out the door as I approached and flung her arms out to me. "So good to see you, honey."

I embraced my mother. "Mom, how long have you been here?"

"Not long. We found the spare key where you always left it and we let ourselves in."

"Well, if it isn't Winifred!" My father appeared at the door. He was a little balder and heavier than the last time I had seen him, but when he smiled there was that familiar youthful twinkle in his blue eyes.

"Dad!" We embraced and went inside. "How's the desert?" I asked.

"Much warmer than it is here," replied my mother, "but we wanted a Michigan Thanksgiving this year."

"Your mother's just saying that," teased my father. "Actually, she's here checking up on you, as usual."

116

"You're looking much better," said my mother.

"And we've heard from Wally that you've been dating a chemistry teacher." My father winked. I smiled briefly, wondering just what it was my brother had written to them about George.

"Oh, by the way, dear," said my mother, "a woman called just a little while ago. I wasn't quite sure of the name she gave me."

Then I remembered that I had promised to help Rob's mother find a new housekeeper. It had crossed my mind several times that day, yet too many distractions had prevented me from actually doing anything about the situation. "Oh, that must have been Mrs. Pelton," I said as I took off my coat.

"Why, yes." My mother looked startled. "Tell me, is this the same Pelton family as..."

"Yes, Mom." I smiled because I knew what my mother was remembering in the back of her mind. "I'd better call her right away."

My mother had already started fixing dinner and resumed her work in the kitchen as I dialed the number at Pelton Manor. I waited a long time before someone answered. It was Marcia.

"Oh, ye-es," Marcia replied after I asked for her mother-in-law. "Well, Irene went out. I don't know when she'll be home, but she did try to reach you this afternoon."

"Tell her I'm sorry I couldn't make it over today," I explained. "I just forgot all about finding someone to take Mrs. McCloskey's place. Tell her I'll get in touch with her tomorrow for sure."

"Whatever," Marcia said indifferently. "Goodbye."

I hung up, unimpressed with Marcia's attitude. I spent the evening enjoying the company of my parents and catching up on all the family news. How wonderful it was to hear the sound of voices and laughter echoing the walls of my house again.

MOST OF Tuesday morning I spent on the telephone, calling agencies and trying to locate a housekeeper for Mrs.

Pelton. I was aware of others working around me, meeting the deadlines before the paper went to press. Because we were going to be closed for Thanksgiving, the publication date had been moved up to Wednesday. I felt guilty not doing my share and was almost ready to give up on the whole housekeeping matter when I finally found a woman who would agree to have an interview at the manor.

"Mrs. Florence Hesselgesser," I scribbled as I talked into the receiver. "And her number..." I scribbled that down too, then said, "Thank you very much. I'll telephone Mrs. Pelton right away. Oh... what's that?"

"She can't start until after Thanksgiving weekend," said the lady at the agency.

"She can't?" I knew Irene Pelton would be disappointed.

"But she'll have to do, Mrs. Grant. There's nobody else available at this time."

After I hung up, I wondered what Irene's reaction would be to learn she wouldn't have a housekeeper until Monday.

It was close to the lunch hour and my stomach began giving me hunger pangs. As I dialed the number to Pelton Manor, I recognized a familiar face in the door to the office. I smiled up at George.

"Hello." It was Irene Pelton who answered.

"Mrs. Pelton, this is Winnie. I've found a housekeeper for you."

"Well, it's about time. You don't know what a relief that is."

I hesitated. "But there is one thing..."

"Oh? What is that?"

I then explained about Mrs. Hesselgesser not being able to start until next week. I knew Irene would be upset and she was. I told her there was nothing I could do about it, and tried to impress upon her the effort and time I had put into this for her. Irene asked if I had heard anything from Rob, which I hadn't, then we said goodbye and hung up.

"George, how are you?" I grinned up at him as he approached my desk.

"Not too bad. And you?"

"I can't complain."

"I don't suppose you're free to have lunch?"

"Well, as a matter of fact, I am, George. JoAnn stayed home today. She wasn't feeling too well, so I'd be very happy to have lunch with you." I got up and went over to get my coat.

"Don't bother asking me first," Marion called out. She pulled out a drawer at the filing cabinet and thumbed through folders.

I stopped. "Oh, Marion, I'm sorry. Did you have plans?"

Marion flashed a smile. "No, you go ahead."

I couldn't help feeling ashamed. I had contributed the least to the paper today, and here I was the first to go on my lunch hour.

"This is really an unexpected surprise," I told George in the elevator. "How did you get away from school?"

"I wheedled a bit. Hey, I've missed you."

I didn't say anything. The elevator door opened and we stepped out.

"I thought of calling you," he continued, "but I figured you wanted some time to yourself for a change. You know, some time in which to think things over. I realize now I was moving too fast."

Outside the air was cold as we headed for George's car parked near the corner.

"Anyway, the truth is, Fred, I had to give myself a break and see you. So, where do you want to eat?"

We had lunch downtown and I found myself enjoying George's company again. I told him about my parents being back in town, how they were spending the week with me, but I said nothing about Rob or Pelton Manor.

He asked me what I had been doing without him around, but I shrugged it off as best I could. I didn't feel ready to tell George about my renewed relationship with Rob. I just couldn't bring myself to tell him, although I realized, as JoAnn had said, George would have to find out about it sooner or later. Right now I only wanted to sit and laugh and be entertained for the hour that I was away from the demands of the paper.

"Hey, I'd really like to meet your mom and dad," George said. I had only been half-listening because I had spotted Marcia Pelton's blonde head across the crowded dining room. Marcia had been staring at me and, just as I noticed her, Marcia quickly turned away.

"Well, what do you say?" asked George.

I looked at him blankly. "About what?"

"About tonight, Fred."

"Sure, George." I craned my neck to see over the tops of heads that separated me from Marcia Pelton. The next minute, Marcia stood up with a man at the same table, who was well dressed and attractive. As they moved toward the cashier, he put his arm around Marcia's waist. Marcia turned to look at me again, then abruptly shifted her gaze.

"Hey, what's so interesting?" asked George.

"Oh, nothing. Just somebody I know."

"Why don't you go over and say hi?"

I lifted my coffee cup to my lips. "No. She's leaving, anyway. Now what were you saying about tonight?"

"I thought you could introduce me to your parents." He grinned. "Haven't you been listening?"

My eyes followed Marcia out the door. I wondered if I should have smiled or waved. Anyway, it didn't matter. What concern of mine was it who Marcia had lunch with?

"What time would be best for me to come over?" George asked after he had driven me back to the office.

"I don't know," I replied. "What time do you think would be best?"

"Probably after dinner?"

"Right."

"Okay, then, I'll be over at seven."

As I walked away from him, I wanted to kick myself. How had I let George talk me into having him come over to meet my parents?

21

Questions

"HOW ARE you recently acquainted with Mrs. Pelton?" My mother and I were cleaning up the kitchen after the meal when the question popped up spontaneously. I could tell, by the way my mother asked, that the question had been on her mind since last night. I knew she was remembering my sixteenth summer, when she had coped with a teen-age daughter having her first love fits.

"It started with an article I wrote for the *Star*," I explained. I then told my mother about the interview at the manor, hesitant to reveal any more and wondering how much she had guessed.

"I wonder whatever happened to that nice boy..."

I looked up at my mother curiously.

"What was his name..." she continued.

"You mean Rob?" I wiped a cup and placed it on the shelf.

"Yes, Rob." She had known it all along, I could tell.

"I hear he's in Connecticut," I replied. "He's quite successful, a professor at the university."

"Oh? How interesting."

We had played our little game long enough. I was just going to reveal to my mother what had happened to me in the last week concerning Rob when George arrived.

My parents were delighted with George's character. I could have enjoyed the evening more had I not been so tired, but by nine o'clock my eyes were starting to droop. I hoped George would notice and take the hint, but he had gotten into a discussion about mole theory with my father. I knew it would probably go on for at least another half hour. My mother could see that I was just about ready to doze off in my chair.

"If we're keeping you up, Winnie, why don't you just go to bed?" she suggested. "You look tired and I know you have to get up in the morning." She had said it as a hint to my father, but he was too absorbed in the chemical discussion with George.

I sighed. "I think I can last a few minutes yet, Mom."

It was then that the telephone rang. I got up to answer it. George and my father kept right on with their discussion.

"Winnie?"

"Oh." I was suddenly wide awake. It was Rob. "Hello. Where are you?"

"I'm calling from Connecticut."

"Just a minute." I put my hand over the mouthpiece. "Mom, I'm going to take this call in the bedroom."

My mother got up and took the phone while I hurried into my room and picked up the extension. I waited until I heard the click of the other phone being placed in its cradle. "Rob, it's so good to hear your voice."

"What's going on? Are you throwing a party?"

I explained about my parents being there. "When are you coming back to Michigan?"

"Not just yet," he said.

"Not even for Thanksgiving?" I couldn't hide my disappointment. Surely Rob's university had Thanksgiving break like everybody else. Why did he have to be gone?

"Listen, one of the reasons I called is about my sister Rose. She's left home."

"What?"

Rob then explained that his mother had called him with the news. Apparently they'd had a fight and Rose had been provoked enough to pack her things.

"Do you know where she went?" I asked.

"No, I was hoping you might."

I remembered that Rose had seemed depressed last Sunday night when she had stopped by to see me. I mentioned Rose's visit to Rob and added, "She was rather upset about some dreams she's been having."

"What dreams?"

I then told him about Rose dreaming about Benjamin. I also told him Rose thought Benjamin's death had been caused by someone else. "Do you have any idea who might have wanted to kill your brother?" I asked.

"Absolutely not," said Rob. "Why would anyone want Ben dead? Winnie, there were only three people in the house that night besides Ben. Just who does Rose suspect? My mother? Marcia? She must be out of her mind. No one else was in the house that night."

"What about the housekeeper?" I asked. "Wasn't there one living at the manor last spring?"

"No." He sounded perturbed. "Actually, I really don't know."

"I think I'll check," I suggested.

"Listen to me," said Rob. "Nobody murdered Benjamin. Why are you getting so worked up about this?"

I wasn't worked up. But Rob wasn't exactly calm. "Well, there's something strange about it all," I insisted. "It's like somebody's hiding something. Don't you think so?"

Rob sighed. "No, I don't."

"Okay, then, how about your father? Haven't you ever wondered about the circumstances of *his* death?"

"I suppose I have, but listen to me, Winnie. Rose's concerns are all blown up out of proportion. She's making a mountain out of a mole hill. I really think it's best if we forget it and leave things alone."

"Leave what things alone?" I couldn't believe that Rob was keeping something from me. "Do you know something that Rose doesn't?"

"Of course not." Rob's voice had become strained. "I could just tell you it's none of your business, but..." There was a silence, then he said, "but I love you."

All turbulence within me quieted at his words. I relaxed. "You know I love you too." Then I said, "I understand. You're right. None of this is any of my business. Maybe I'm being a snoop."

Rob changed the subject. "I heard that Mrs. McCloskey quit."

I told him I was helping his mother get a new housekeeper and he thanked me. We talked a few minutes longer and reluctantly said our good-nights before we hung up.

I had been so happy that he had called, but somehow was left with a disturbed feeling. What did Rob know about his family that he didn't want me to know? It sounded as if he objected to my asking questions. Most upsetting, though, was learning about Rose. Where was she? What had been said to cause her to leave home? I could well imagine just by remembering how Irene had embarrassed Rose in front of me last weekend at the manor.

When I returned to the living room, the chemical discussion was still going, but my mother finally interrupted it. She insisted that the men were keeping me up, so George said good-night to everyone and left. I went straight to bed, but lay awake for a long while.

22

That Man Again

"COME ON in, JoAnn. It's good to see you again." My mother's voice trailed into the bedroom, where I ran the brush one last time through my hair. JoAnn's car hadn't started again this morning and she had called for a ride to work.

"Are you feeling better, Jo?" I asked as I entered the room.

"Much better," JoAnn replied. "It was just a little flu bug, I'm sure. Better dress warm. It's snowing out."

"Really?" My mother peeked out the draperies. "Oh, just a few flurries."

"Well, you and Dad have a good day." I kissed my mother on the cheek.

"We will, honey. We thought we'd drive out to see Ken and Phyllis this afternoon."

JoAnn and I left the house.

"I can't believe we have all this catching up to do," remarked JoAnn on the way to work. "It's been since Monday that we've talked to one another. How's Rob?"

I filled her in briefly about Rob still being in Connecticut, then asked if JoAnn was still seeing her psychologist friend.

JoAnn seemed to stiffen a little. "Yes," she said.

"Well," I teased, "is it love?"

"I'm afraid so."

"What do you mean you're *afraid* so? When are you going to introduce him to me?"

JoAnn grimaced. "Are you sure you want to meet him?"

I laughed. "Come on, Jo. A week ago you were dying for me to meet him. What happened?"

JoAnn sighed. "If you must know, I'm thinking about breaking it off with him."

"Why?"

"I found out something."

I could guess just what it was. JoAnn's boyfriend was a married man. JoAnn confessed I had guessed correctly.

"How do you feel about him now that you know?"

"I don't know."

"How did you find out? Did you call his house and his wife answered?"

"No, he told me."

We got out of the car and started walking toward our office building.

"He wants to keep on seeing me," continued JoAnn, "but I'm not sure it's the right thing to do. I wish I'd never gotten involved."

I didn't know what to say to her, so we parted on our floor after agreeing to have lunch together.

I called Pelton Manor that morning to find out if they had heard anything from Rose.

"No, we haven't heard anything from her," Irene said. "Oh dear, what am I going to do? No housekeeper, and with Thanksgiving *tomorrow*."

I offered to go over to the manor and help with some of the cleaning until the day Mrs. Hesselgesser arrived.

"That's very sweet of you, Winnie, but it's not necessary. Aunt Pearl and Aunt Ophelia have invited us over. They are planning to fix dinner for us. When I offered to let them fix it here, they declined. I can't imagine why not. After all, there's much more room here." She sighed. "I only wish Rob could come home. There's not much family left now that Rose is gone."

"I'm glad the aunts can help out," I said.

"Why don't you join us tomorrow, too?" asked Irene.

126

"Thank you, but I'm having dinner with my family." I then explained how my parents had driven up from Arizona.

"Of course, dear," said Irene. "That will be nice for you."

The morning was busy, and the afternoon passed quickly. I was glad to look forward to a four-day weekend. On the way home from work, JoAnn wanted to stop at the store for a few groceries, so we drove to the neighborhood market.

The store was crowded with lots of people shopping for their last-minute holiday items. JoAnn was picking out a head of lettuce when I noticed Shirley Peterson rolling a cart down the produce aisle. I went over to her.

"Hi, Winnie." Shirley seemed surprised to see me.

"How's Greg doing with the paper route?" I asked.

By this time JoAnn had noticed us and came over with her basket. She and Shirley exchanged greetings.

"He delivered the paper to the Peltons today without any trouble at all," Shirley said. "All his friends are looking up to him again."

"I'm glad to hear that," I replied.

Shirley smiled. "Actually, Winnie, I'm glad he's over this ghost business. He had me worried." She wanted to talk on and on, but I thought of something I wanted to ask.

"Shirley, didn't you mention to me that a friend of your mother's worked for the Peltons?"

"Why, yes, Mrs. McCloskey."

"Is there some way I can get in touch with her?"

"Well, I'm sure if you telephone the Peltons..."

"No, no, you see, she quit last weekend."

"Oh? I wasn't aware of that." Shirley grew more curious by the second. "Why did she quit?"

"Well, I'm not really sure," I lied, "but I would like to get in touch with her—to see if I can get her to go back to work there."

JoAnn came to the rescue. "Winnie's been helping Mrs. Pelton try to find a new housekeeper," she explained.

"Oh, I see." Shirley smiled. "Well, I'm sure that my mother would know where she is. Here, I'll give you her number and you can call her when you get home."

"Thanks so much." I found a pen and a piece of scrap paper in my purse and Shirley jotted down her mother's phone number.

"Do you really think you can get her to go back?" JoAnn asked on our way out to the car.

"No, but I thought I might learn something from her. There's been something weird going on in that house."

JoAnn stopped suddenly and almost dropped her bag of groceries. "Look over there! What's that man doing?"

I saw somebody looking into the window of my car in the parking lot. My mouth dropped open as I recognized the cap and the beard and the sheepskin coat. It was the same heavy, ruddy-faced man who had been watching me in the bar when I had been out with Rob. The moment he noticed us, the man turned his back and walked away.

I thrust my bag into JoAnn's arms and she almost lost her balance.

"Winnie!"

"Wait!" I called out. I started to run after the man. He wouldn't turn around. "Please come back," I shouted. "Sir, I just want to..." It was no use. He leaped over a fence and disappeared around the corner of a building.

JoAnn caught up with me. "Who was he?"

"I have no idea, but I've seen him a couple of times before. Once in the bar last Friday night, and once..." I grabbed my bag from JoAnn. "...You know, I can't figure it out. I've seen him some other place recently."

"Winnie, I think you should call the police."

"Why? He hasn't done anything." We got into the car.

"You mean *yet*," she added.

"I wonder why he's..." I looked at JoAnn's concerned face. My friend tilted her glasses. "I wonder if he's been following me."

"What?"

I told JoAnn about how I was sure a car had followed me

after I left Pelton Manor that rainy evening that I had been invited over to dinner. Then I remembered that I had felt someone had been in the woods following me that Tuesday afternoon I had interviewed the old aunts at their cottage.

"Winnie, this is scary."

I tried to blow it off. "It's probably my imagination."

"Then why was he snooping around by your car?"

"I don't know. Maybe he likes old Dodges."

When I got home, my parents hadn't returned yet. I put the groceries away, then dialed the number on the slip of paper Shirley Peterson had given me. A woman whom I assumed to be Shirley's mother answered. I gave my name and explained that I wished to contact Mrs. McCloskey.

"Clara McCloskey?" asked the woman.

"I don't know her first name," I admitted, "but she was employed by the Peltons."

Shirley's mother said that Mrs. McCloskey was staying with her sister and brother-in-law, and gave me an address across town. I thanked her, then hung up. I decided to try and see Mrs. McCloskey tonight. With tomorrow being a holiday, I didn't want to disturb her, and I just couldn't wait until Friday to get some answers.

I was scribbling a note to explain where I was going, so my parents wouldn't worry, when the telephone rang. When I picked it up and said hello, I heard a click at the other end. Before I could repeat myself, the person hung up. A twinge of uncertainty caused a moment of panic. What if it was that man with the beard, checking to see if I was home? Grabbing my coat and keys, I flew out the door to my car.

23

Irene's Strange Behavior

IT WAS already dark when I found the address of Mrs. McCloskey's sister. I walked up to the porch and knocked on the door. Mrs. McCloskey answered and recognized me at once. "Why, Mrs. Grant! Whatever... ? Come in."

As I stepped into the living room I could smell dinner cooking. "Did I come at a bad time?"

"No, dear. I'm just rather surprised to see you."

I decided to get right to the point. "Mrs. McCloskey, I came to talk with you."

"Well, come in. We can talk in the kitchen." She led me through a narrow hallway and into a small kitchen where the floor slanted a little, probably because of the age and condition of the house. "I hope nothing is wrong," said Mrs. McCloskey.

"Everything's fine at the manor, except that Rose has left home and nobody's heard from her."

"Oh dear." Mrs. McCloskey shook her head in dismay, then beckoned for me to sit down at the kitchen table. "I'll fix us some coffee and we can talk. My sister is sleeping in the bedroom."

"Mrs. Pelton was really upset after you left," I said.

"Was she? Well..."

"You wouldn't consider going back, would you?"

"Not on your life! Mrs. Grant, I refuse to work in a crazy woman's house."

I hated to sound nosy, but I asked, "Why? What did she do

to make you leave?"

Mrs. McCloskey turned on the coffee maker, then seated herself across the table. "Well, it wasn't one particular thing. I told you how I felt about being in that house—and about seeing Benjamin's spirit."

I nodded.

She went on. "Well, it happened Sunday morning. But before I tell you about that, let me tell you another thing. It was the way Mrs. Irene was always disappearing."

"Disappearing? What do you mean?"

"Oh, I'd go to the store a lot for Mrs. Irene and do errands for her. Many times when I returned, she'd be gone—just out of sight—and I could never figure out where she went. It always happened when everyone was gone from the house."

"Hm."

"All of a sudden, she'd come into the kitchen or wherever I'd be—as if she'd been around all along—and I'd say to her, 'Mrs. Irene, where were you? I came home and you weren't anywhere. I looked all over for you and called your name...' and she'd tell me she had just left the house for a few minutes. 'Left where?' I'd ask, and she'd say, 'Oh, just out for a walk.' But it gets cold out this time of year, Mrs. Grant, and she never took her coat. I checked!"

"That's odd," I remarked. "Now tell me what happened Sunday morning."

"Sunday," resumed Mrs. McCloskey, "Mrs. Irene and Marcia had gone off to visit Benjamin's and Otto's graves at the cemetery. It's only a short walk, you know, and they go there often to pay their respects.

"Anyway, I had just started on my way to church when I remembered I forgot my cathedral veil. So, I returned to the house to get it and couldn't find it. Well, I thought I'd go upstairs and borrow one of Mrs. Irene's. I knew she wouldn't mind. Besides, she and Marcia weren't there anyway.

"Well, I got upstairs when I heard footsteps above me. It startled me something horrible, and I went from Mrs. Irene's room into the hall and stood listening to see if I could hear more. There came these thuds from the ceiling, the same ones I've heard on occasion while changing linens in the upstairs bedrooms.

"Then I heard footsteps coming down the stairway from the third floor, so I quickly ran into Rosie's room and hid behind the door. A glass dropped somewhere and broke on the floor, and then I heard Mrs. Irene's voice. She mumbled something and then picked up the broken glass.

"I just waited there in Rosie's room, afraid to show myself. It seemed like an hour that I waited there. Then, when I was sure Mrs. Irene was in another part of the house, I hurried downstairs and gathered up my things and left."

I was intrigued by Mrs. McCloskey's story. "Mrs. McCloskey, do you have any idea why Mrs. Pelton was up on the third floor? I thought it was all boarded up."

"It's supposed to be," she insisted. Mrs. McCloskey poured us each a cup of coffee. "I don't understand it. She and Marcia left for the cemetery just before I left for church."

"Apparently she came back after she was sure you had gone," I surmised. "You didn't get a look at her when she came down those stairs?"

"No. I made certain to stay hidden."

"There must be something up there," I said, "something she doesn't want anyone to know about."

"All those times I thought she had disappeared," added Mrs. McCloskey, "she could have been upstairs on that third floor—and didn't want to come down because she knew I was home. No, I'm not going back, Mrs. Grant. I'm not working for that crazy woman anymore."

I asked Mrs. McCloskey what she knew of Benjamin's death and the housekeeper gave only the facts I already knew. "No, the Peltons didn't have a housekeeper living in the manor at that time," she said in answer to my question. "They probably didn't need one then. My sister-in-law used to do the housecleaning there twice a week. Before she lost her husband,

Mrs. Irene was perfectly capable of running the manor by herself."

After I finished my coffee, I told Mrs. McCloskey I had to be getting home and thanked her for the visit. Then I drove home in the dark, wondering how I could find out why Irene Pelton made secret trips up to the third floor.

I wondered if I should telephone Rob. I decided against it. He had been so negative on the phone last night. I figured I'd wait until I heard from him again. Maybe then I'd have more information.

24

Spider Lake

THURSDAY MORNING my mother and I got up early to stuff the turkey and prepare for our feast. My brother and his wife had telephoned last night with the news that they had decided to drive over from Pontiac. When they arrived around noon with their two kids, there was a spirited reunion between the older couple and their grandchildren.

The day turned out to be a busy one with my father and Wally absorbed in TV football and my mother, sister-in-law and I preoccupied with kitchen duties. My niece and nephew ran in and out of the house. My humble domain was filled with lively sounds that made me wonder what it would have been like had Alan and I had any children. I often wished we had, so that there would be a piece of Alan left in the world. But, considering how things had turned out, I was actually grateful I didn't have to raise any alone.

Throughout the afternoon I wondered what kind of Thanksgiving Rob was having all by himself. I missed him terribly. I even thought about George once or twice. George had called the night before, but I had told him not to come over because I was too tired. I hadn't even thought to ask him what he was doing for the holiday, whether he had anywhere to go for dinner or not. Now I felt a little guilty about George being alone on Thanksgiving.

At the end of the day, Wally and his wife packed their

sleepy kids into their car and left. They had a long drive home and refused my invitation for them to spend the night.

Friday morning I slept late, since the office was closed. The ringing of the telephone roused me and I groped across my bed to answer it. When I heard Rob's voice, I slid up in bed and sat against my pillow. "Rob, where are you?"

"I'm back in Spundale," he said. "I got in early this morning. Did you have a nice Thanksgiving?"

I assured him I had and asked about Rose.

"Still no word from her," said Rob. When I sighed, he seemed to sense my concern for his sister. "Hey, cheer up. Rose is a big girl. She knows how to take care of herself. Besides, I've got an idea."

"What is it?"

"Let's take a trip up north today."

"What?" I sat up more and saw that my radio clock said nine thirty-two. I couldn't believe I had slept this late.

"The truth is," Rob continued, "I've been doing a lot of thinking since we talked the other night, and I'd like to take a trip up to Spider Lake and look into the matter regarding my father." After a pause, he asked, "Do you want to come along?"

I explained how I had wanted to spend the day with my parents, but decided to go with Rob instead. I knew my folks would be disappointed, but I missed Rob terribly. I wanted to be with him.

"How soon should I be ready?"

"I'll be over to pick you up at eleven," said Rob.

"Have you told your mother you're going?" I asked.

"No. I thought it might upset her," Rob replied.

By the time I was dressed, my parents had gotten up and my mother was already in the kitchen frying eggs.

"You don't have to go to work, do you?" asked my father in reference to the phone call.

"Oh no," I replied, "but I hope you don't mind if I go away for the day. Rob Pelton will be over at eleven. We're taking a drive up north."

"*Who's* coming over?" asked my mother.

"Rob Pelton," my father repeated.

When I looked at my mother, I saw a smile. I could tell my mother had suspected. We hadn't talked at all about my seeing Rob again, yet my mother had a talent for reading between the lines. "Of course, honey." She flipped an egg in the pan. "You go on. We still have tomorrow to spend together."

Rob showed up at eleven, as promised. I introduced him briefly to my parents and then we began the long drive to Spider Lake Resort.

"Your parents remembered me," said Rob.

I snuggled closer to him. "Of course, how could they forget?"

It felt so good to be with him again, so right.

Rob found my hand and gripped it as he smiled down at me. "Miss me?"

I laid my head against his shoulder. "Gobs."

He laughed. "I haven't heard anyone say that in... ten years." It had been our pet expression that special summer together. The memory of it made me smile.

I then asked Rob what made him decide to take this trip. "What do you expect to find out about your father?"

"That I don't know yet," he told me. "I got to thinking after you told me what Rose said to you—and in the back of my mind I've always wondered about the true circumstances of my father's death. I aim to get to the bottom of it all, and the only place to start is Spider Lake, where he died."

I then told him how I had been to see Mrs. McCloskey and disclosed what the woman had told me about his mother. He looked bewildered and admitted that it was odd Irene should be making secret trips upstairs.

"Of course, Mrs. McCloskey might be mistaken," said Rob. "I can't think of any reason why my mother would go up there except for something she had put away. That glass she dropped was probably some family heirloom of some kind."

I dozed off during the last half hour of the journey. When I awoke, we were on a back road heading toward the Spider

Lake resort area. It was beautiful country, even for that drab time of year after the trees have been stripped of their colorful leaves.

The Spider Lake convalescent home was a rather extravagant facility for elderly people who had money and could afford the luxury of being cared for in such a scenic spot.

Otto Pelton had been an invalid after his stroke. Rob explained that his mother had placed his father into this home because she had only wanted the best for her husband, and this resort was the best money could buy. It hadn't mattered to her that it was located so far from Spundale. She didn't mind having to travel that far to visit him in the short weeks he had lived.

Rob parked the car and as we made our way, hand in hand, to the resort office, we watched elderly people sitting in chairs along the lakeshore. It was chilly, but the sun had come out and the patients seemed to enjoy being outside. One elderly man was standing over a pier with a fishing rod.

"Have you been here before?" I asked Rob.

"No." He stared at the ground as we walked. "I never saw my father alive after Ben's funeral."

We entered the office. A nurse came in from hearing the tinkling of the bell on the door. Rob introduced himself and explained why we had come. The nurse went to a filing cabinet and searched for a couple of minutes, then returned with a folder containing the records they had on Otto Pelton.

"He was here for three weeks, it says," the nurse said. "He was admitted on July 7 and he died on July 28." She looked at Rob and waved her finger. "I remember Mr. Pelton. I'm sure I do. He was recovering from a stroke, I believe. We were so saddened to hear he had passed away."

Rob cleared his throat. "Do you suppose we could have a word with the doctor in charge?"

The nurse closed the file. "Well, unfortunately, Dr. Gamble is no longer with us. You see, he left last summer and took up private practice in Grand Rapids."

"Can you tell me anything else about my father?" asked Rob. "What else do you remember about him?"

The nurse thought a minute. "Well, I remember Mrs. Pelton coming to see him. She usually came twice a week. And I remember the day he died. I came in that morning and he was gone. I was told he had died in the night. Of course, Mrs. Pelton was very upset. We all were, for that matter."

The nurse gave Rob the name and address of Dr. Gamble in Grand Rapids. Then, because there was nothing more we could find out, we left.

It was starting to get dark as we headed for the car. "It's only about an hour out of our way," Rob said as we headed back down the country road from Spider Lake. "What do you think?"

I realized it didn't matter what I thought. If Rob thought there was something more to learn from this doctor who had attended his father, then it was worth going to see him. We headed for Grand Rapids.

It was close to seven o'clock when we arrived in the city and we were starved, so we stopped at a restaurant and ate a quick supper. Rob bought a city map with which to find the doctor's residence.

"It's quite possible he may not even be home," said Rob as he drove. I searched the street signs with the open map in my lap. We did manage to find the house and the lights were on, so we stopped.

The doctor's wife answered the door when we rang and she invited us in. I noticed that it was a very luxurious home.

"Dr. Gamble." Rob reached out his hand as an elderly man with curly white hair and wire-rimmed glasses entered the room. He shook Rob's hand.

"What can I do for you, young man?"

"Well, I hope to find out something about a patient you took care of up at Spider Lake."

The doctor smiled in a haughty fashion. "I'm sorry, but I do not give out such information. I strongly feel my cases are confidential."

"Oh, you don't understand." I stepped forward. "He is referring to his father, Otto Pelton. He was a patient of yours last July at Spider Lake."

The doctor's face had strangely blanched and he seemed to be staring right through us at blank space.

"My father died last July 28," continued Rob. "I just wanted to find out a few facts regarding his death."

The doctor gripped the back of a chair. "I have nothing to tell you."

"But you did handle his case, didn't you?" asked Rob.

"I'd rather not discuss it." The doctor's voice had hardened.

"Why not?" I asked. "What's wrong?"

"I'd like you to leave," Dr. Gamble told us.

"All I want to know is what caused his death," said Rob. "Was it due to his stroke or something else?"

"Jean!" the doctor called.

"You *did* sign his death certificate, didn't you?" I felt something was terribly wrong here.

The doctor pulled at his chin. "Well, yes I did, I suppose I did." His wife entered the room to see what he wanted. "Jean, see them out." At that, he quickly left the room and his wife eyed Rob and me, then led us to the door.

On our way back to the car, Rob put his arm around me. We were too baffled to speak until we were in the car and headed for the highway once again.

"That was very strange," I said. "I wonder what upset him so much."

Rob sighed. "So do I."

I offered to help drive back to Spundale because Rob looked very tired, but he insisted on driving the rest of the way. In two hours we were back in our hometown and Rob pulled his car into my driveway. The kitchen light was the only light on in my house. It was well after eleven o'clock and I assumed my parents had already gone to bed.

Rob drew me close to him and I felt warm and secure in his arms. "You know," he said, "I drove up to Spider Lake expecting to ease my conscience about my father, but all it did was confuse me more."

I looked at him. "Ease your conscience? Rob, you have no reason to blame yourself for what happened to your father."

He sighed. "I can't help it. It bothers me that I didn't even go to see him."

"But you were away," I reminded him.

Rob held me tighter, then looked into my face and kissed me.

I was so hungry for his kisses. Prickles of arousal surged throughout my body. He nuzzled the back of my neck and his hand moved down between my legs. He sighed deeply and fumbled to undo my zipper. Then his hand slid inside my panties. He was hurried, almost demanding, in his advances. Yet the passion within me was rising steadily with his.

"Wait," I whispered, feeling his breath against my ear. "We can't do this here... in my driveway."

"Where would you like to go?" he asked.

"I don't know." I knew my house certainly was not available to us, at least until after my parents left.

"Let's go to a motel," said Rob.

I pulled away. "A motel?" I pretended to be shocked. "How sleazy."

Rob sat up straight and looked around. "Well, a car is so... so... uncouth."

"My parents will be expecting me," I said softly. "Maybe we shouldn't..."

"Don't care..." He held me tight. "I just know one thing... I want you, Winnie."

I kissed him lightly and smiled. Just then, the back porch light flashed on.

"Oh no," groaned Rob.

"I'd better go in," I told him. I zippered up my pants.

Rob sighed. "It hasn't been like this since..."

"I know." I reached for the door handle. "That's my mother's distress signal. *Her* distress, not mine."

25

Too Many Goodbyes

SATURDAY I spent the day with my parents. We went out to eat that night, so I didn't get a chance to see Rob. Sunday morning there was a teary goodbye with a lot of hugging and kissing, and then my parents boarded their fifth-wheel and departed for Arizona. I really hated to see them drive off. I had quickly gotten used to having someone else around the house, and they weren't planning to drive up for Christmas.

To make matters worse, Rob called to say goodbye. "I hate to do it," he said, "but I have to return to Connecticut, hopefully for the last time." He then explained that the professor for whom he was filling in had not recovered from an illness and they desperately needed him there.

"Why can't they get somebody else?" I whined into the telephone.

"I know it's hard for you to understand," Rob said, "but I do owe the university something for all the years they've given me." After a pause, he added, "If it's any consolation, Winnie, I'm thinking of taking a sabbatical and coming back to Spundale."

After I hung up, I was still dismayed at the news of his leaving again, but cheered up at the prospect of it being the last time he would leave me.

MOST THE afternoon I sat around moping, feeling like a forlorn child and longing for Rob. It only made matters worse to have George call.

"Hi, Fred. What ya been up to?"

"Oh hello, George.'"

"What's wrong, Fred? You sound like you lost your best friend."

I ignored his comment. "How was your Thanksgiving?" I asked.

"At the last minute one of my colleagues from the science department called me up and invited me over to his house. His wife's a great cook—just like you."

"That's good," I said.

"Hey, you sound like you could use some cheering up."

I sniffed. I didn't feel like talking right now.

"How about if I come over?" suggested George.

"No, George, please, not today."

"Well then, we can see that new movie that's in town."

"I don't think so, George."

After a pause, he said, "But then, if you'd rather be by yourself, I can understand." Not even a hint of resentment or hurt feelings. I just couldn't believe anyone could be this patient.

"That's what I want," I told him. "I need to be by myself tonight." Then, feeling a little guilty, I added, "Thank you anyway, George. I appreciate what you're trying to do."

"Maybe I'll see you tomorrow sometime—or whenever," he replied.

"Whenever."

"Bye, Fred."

"Goodbye."

As I hung up the phone, I thought of how many goodbyes had been said that day and felt so depressed I wanted to cry. But no tears came.

26

The Closet Incident

MONDAY MORNING I left the office at nine-thirty to drive over to Pelton Manor. Irene had called me and asked me to be there when the new housekeeper came. Why Irene needed me there was beyond my wildest guess. Apparently, she figured that since I had located the new housekeeper, I should also be the one to welcome her. Although I felt obligated to my job, Mr. Pendergast had been more than generous in letting me go.

Irene greeted me at the door. "I'm relieved you could come. The new housekeeper is already here. She's putting her things in her room."

"Well, do you think you'll like her?" I asked.

Irene shrugged. "She'll do. By the way, Winnie..." Irene's countenance darkened. "I was rather upset when I learned you had gone with Rob up north Friday."

I was startled. Irene tried to keep calm, but there was a nervous edge in her voice, almost a scolding tone. "Oh, then Rob told you we went," I said.

"Yes. Apparently he wanted to know a few things about Otto." She ushered me into the living room. "But never mind, dear. I was hoping you could help Mrs. Hesselgesser get started. I haven't been feeling well."

"I'm sorry to hear that," I said, then asked if there had been any word from Rose.

"No. None. You wait here. I'll go see what's taking that woman so long to put her things away." Irene hurried out.

I wandered over to one of the huge Victorian windows to look out at the front lawn when I heard footsteps behind me and turned and saw Marcia.

"What are you doing here?" Marcia eyed me from head to toe.

Somehow I felt embarrassed. "Mrs. Pelton wants me to help with the new housekeeper."

"Hmph. I'm glad she didn't ask me." Marcia sauntered over to the fireplace and picked up a poker to stir up the coals. A glow of orange showed that there had been a fire blazing that morning.

I thought of something to ask her. "Marcia, do you ever feel cold?"

Marcia turned and scowled.

I couldn't help smiling at my impulsive choice of words. "I know this might sound kind of silly," I said, "but do you ever hear strange sounds?"

"What?" She returned the poker to its stand and took a seat in one of the armchairs. I could tell she was annoyed.

"You know — scrapings or bumps in the night," I continued.

Marcia looked insulted. "No! Besides, I don't believe in any of that stuff."

"What stuff?"

"About haunted houses and spirits, of all things." She picked up a paperback from the table next to her. "And don't ask me anything more, Winnie. I've heard enough from the aunts to last me a lifetime."

I shrugged and turned back to stare out the window. Just then, Irene entered with Mrs. Hesselgesser, a small egg of a woman with dark hair that looked like it had been cut by placing a bowl over her head. Her face was wrinkled and when she smiled, it looked more like she was getting ready to cry.

"I'd like you to meet Mrs. Grant," said Irene.

"Hello, Mrs. Hesselgesser."

"Oh no, please call me Florence. It's much easier."

"All right."

"Florence," said Irene, "I want you to go with Winnie now and she'll show you the house. Meanwhile, I'll see what we need from the store, so you can go out later today."

"By the way, Winnie," rang out Marcia's voice from the chair. "Who was that charming man you were with the other day?"

I could feel Irene staring at me curiously and a pang of anger swelled within me.

"You know—at the restaurant I saw you in downtown," Marcia continued. "My, but he was attractive. Blond hair, blue eyes, and the two of you sure looked cozy. And with Rob out of town—how convenient."

"Marcia!" It was the first harsh word I had heard Irene give her daughter-in-law.

"What, Irene?"

"I don't think that was any of your business."

"Well, I just wanted to know. I'd kind of like a crack at him myself."

Irene seemed to quiver and I thought she was about to reproach Marcia again, but instead she turned to me. "Go on, dear." She motioned toward the hallway.

I led Mrs. Hesselgesser up the stairs and showed her the bedrooms and baths. Then we decided to make the beds. I offered to get the sheets from the linen closet. In a way, I was really enjoying this, being in the manor and helping with making the beds. It was almost like being the mistress of the estate.

I went downstairs and met Marcia in the hall. "Where's the linen closet?" I asked.

Marcia pointed toward it, then retreated to the library. I walked over to the closet and opened the door. Suddenly, something fell out. I cried out and stepped aside just in time to avoid being hit.

"What is it? What happened?" Irene ran in from the dining

room after she heard the clatter. She gasped. "Winnie! Are you all right?"

A large brass vase lay on the carpet next to the closet. If I hadn't been so quick, it would have fallen right on my head. "All I did was open the door," I explained, "and it fell out."

The next moment, Marcia had arrived and seemed to piece together the situation in her mind.

"Why, that was my grandmother's old vase," said Irene. "Whatever was it doing up there?" She squatted down to pick it up. Then she handed it to me. It was even heavier than it looked, and I gave it back to Irene. I felt a rush of blood as my heart began to race.

"My dear, you could have been hurt!"

I looked at Marcia, who immediately turned away and ran up the staircase.

"I'm all right," I said. Most likely, the vase had fallen by accident, but I had a dreadful feeling that someone had planted it there on purpose.

"I'll put on some tea," suggested Irene.

"We'll finish making the beds first." I collected the needed linens, then started up the stairs again. I found Mrs. Hesselgesser standing and staring up at the narrow stairway that led to the third floor.

"What's up there?" she asked me.

"The third floor."

"Do I have to clean up there, too?"

"Oh no, Florence. Mrs. Pelton doesn't let anyone go up there." I was aware of Marcia listening in her room and so I didn't want to say anything more. "Don't worry. There's nothing up there you have to clean."

"Oh, that's good."

"I hope you'll like working for the Peltons," I said.

"I'm sure I will, ma'am. I love mansions."

We were almost done making the beds when Irene called to us from downstairs. "Winnie! Florence! The tea is ready!"

"Okay, I'm coming!" I shouted from Rose's bedroom.

"*Oh-h,*" whimpered Mrs. Hesselgesser and clutched her back.

"What is it?" I asked.

The housekeeper tried to smile and her face turned into a prune. "I'm all right, Mrs. Grant. I just have a bad back. I'll be all right in a minute."

"Are you sure?"

"Yes." She grasped my arm and held me. "Please don't tell Mrs. Pelton. I need this job, ma'am, despite my poor health."

"Well, all right. Maybe you'd better go on down and I'll finish up here."

"No, no. I couldn't let you do that," she protested.

"Florence, go on. Tell Mrs. Pelton I'm coming."

"Well... okay, if you insist." Mrs. Hesselgesser shuffled out of the room. I began tucking and smoothing again. With the amount of housework Mrs. Hesselgesser would have in the manor, I wondered how long the woman would stay.

I began thinking of Rose, because this was her room, and wondered where she could be. What if something had happened to her? I wished Rose would get in touch with either Rob or myself.

I stood up when I heard a loud commotion in the hall. Then I heard Mrs. Hesselgesser scream and scream. I bolted out of the bedroom to see what was the matter, then gasped as I stood at the top of the staircase and looked down.

27

Tragedy

THE HOUSEKEEPER lay sprawled in a twisted heap at the bottom of the steps, writhing in pain.

"Oh, dear God!" cried Marcia. She had just come out of her room.

I didn't wait another moment. I gripped the rail and hurried down the steps. When I reached the injured housekeeper, the woman lifted her head and gasped as if she couldn't get enough air.

"Somebody call an ambulance!" I shouted.

"Irene! Irene!" Marcia yelled. She rushed down the steps.

Mrs. Hesselgesser's face turned a hideous gray color. Her eyes bulged up at me and, a few seconds later, they fell shut. Her body sank into a heap.

Irene ran in from the kitchen and drew back at the sight.

"Quick! Call the police! An ambulance!" I groped for the housekeeper's wrist to find her pulse. I was aware of Marcia squeezing past me and moving toward the telephone. I couldn't feel a pulse at all.

"What happened?" Irene's voice shook.

"I think she's dead." My voice sounded strange to me.

When the police and ambulance crew arrived several minutes later, I left the housekeeper's side and joined Irene and Marcia in the hallway. We were all in a state of shock.

"She's dead all right," said the paramedic. "Did she have a bad heart?" He looked from Irene to Marcia and me. "She might have survived the fall otherwise."

"We don't know," Marcia mumbled in reply.

"She only started working here this morning," explained Irene.

"It's no wonder she tripped and fell," called a police officer from the top of the staircase. "A section of this carpet was sticking out over the first step. It must have caught her footing."

Something scared me about what he said about the carpet. I remembered the vase in the linen closet. Then I recalled that I could easily have been the first one down the stairs. I might have tripped and fallen in the housekeeper's place.

"Somebody must have accidentally kicked the rug out of place," the officer called down.

"That rug is always coming loose," said Irene.

Marcia stared at her mother-in-law.

"Well, it's time you got it replaced, ma'am." His partner ushered the three of us into the next room as the paramedics began to load Mrs. Hesselgesser's body onto a stretcher. "All right, ladies," he said, "I have a few questions I have to ask you."

The telephone rang and Marcia went to answer it.

"I want you to tell me exactly what happened," the officer said. He pulled out his note pad as I sat down and began telling him what I had heard and how I had found Mrs. Hesselgesser.

"Rob's on the phone," announced Marcia in a weak voice. "He wants to speak to *you*, Winnie."

I left the room. "Rob?" I cried into the receiver. I was sure I was going to cry.

"Was Marcia putting me on?" It was hard to hear him with all the commotion. "Was there some kind of accident?"

My entire body trembled as I swallowed to compose myself. "She... she wasn't putting you on. Wh-when will you be home?"

"I'm catching the next flight," he said. "I should be there this afternoon. Are you all right?"

I couldn't answer. I was fighting tears.

"Don't worry, darling," he continued, "I'll be there as soon as I can."

28

Unfulfilled

I WAS still dazed from the experience at the manor when I returned to the office and reported what had happened to Mr. Pendergast and the staff. They were very sympathetic and insisted I take the rest of the day off. Although I protested, I knew it was the right thing to do and was only too glad to get home.

JoAnn had given me a couple of tranquilizers she had in her purse. Later, she called to see how I was doing.

"Much calmer," I said, although I was feeling rather groggy from the medication.

"Has Rob called yet?" she asked.

"No, but I'm sure he will as soon as he gets in."

"Hey, I have an idea," said JoAnn. "Martin and I were planning to go out for a little while tonight. How about if we stop over and see you a little later? He still would like to meet you."

The idea was agreeable with me. I asked JoAnn if she had decided to keep her affair going.

JoAnn sighed. "Why fight the inevitable?"

Shortly after I talked with JoAnn, Rob's car pulled into my driveway. Peeking out the drapes, I sighed with relief and let the curtain fall back. Everything was going to be all right now that he was back in Spundale.

Rob took me into his arms and led me to the couch. "My poor darling," he crooned. "Tell me how it happened."

As he held me close, I related the events at the manor that morning. I even told about the brass vase falling out of the linen closet and nearly hitting me. "Then when the officer mentioned that section of carpet, it just really made me stop and think. Rob, I could have been dead right now."

"Winnie, Winnie, get a hold of yourself." Rob held me at arm's length. "I want you to know I'm concerned about you. But you've got to know that vase could not have been planted there on purpose. You're letting your imagination get the better of you."

I blinked. "You think it was a mere coincidence?"

He frowned. "Who do you think would attempt to harm you?"

"Well, I know Marcia despises me," I admitted.

Rob sighed. "Marcia... you can't be serious. And I suppose you think she was the one who pushed Benjamin down the stairs the night he died."

"I'm not saying that," I said. "I'm just saying that Marcia does seem to have something against me. She has since the first time I met her. Maybe she's afraid I'll learn something about Benjamin's death that we don't already know."

"Or maybe she's just jealous of you," said Rob.

I sat up straight and stared at him. "Jealous... of *me?*"

Rob kissed my hand and smiled. "You are very beautiful, you know."

I grunted. "But... with her looks and her style... it doesn't make sense." Rob drew me close and his touch began to arouse something in me. Yet I could not put the disturbing fears out of my mind. "No, I think it's more than that," I said. "Certainly she wouldn't go to such extremes just because of ... that's ridiculous, Rob!"

He shrugged. "See, that's my point. She wouldn't harm you. You don't know Marcia well enough is all."

"And you do?"

Rob shook his head. "You're all uptight about this thing. You're paranoid, and it all started from Rose's delusions about Ben and my father."

"Well, Mrs. Hesselgesser's death was no delusion!" I could feel my cheeks getting warm. "Somebody moved that rug out of place for me to trip on. Only because the woman had a bad back did she happen to be the first one down those stairs! And Rob, Marcia was the only one in the house near enough to those stairs to do it!"

"Shh... shh, that's enough. Let's not argue about it right now." He tilted my face up toward his and then kissed me.

I surrendered to the tenderness of his kiss and felt myself relinquish my concerns as a magical cloud of sensation encircled me.

Rob's grip tightened and his kisses grew more passionate. I remembered the intense feelings we had shared a few nights ago in his parked car in my driveway. His kisses now were begging me to submit to his need. I also desired to take the steps that would lead to our love's fulfillment. My breasts tingled as I felt the warmth of his hands brush up beneath my blouse. I let him press my body back upon the couch as his eager hands began to explore my lower parts.

As his hungry mouth moved over my jaw, my neck and my shoulders, shivers of pleasure surfaced, and yet I felt the weight of his body and it was making it hard for me to breathe. I kept telling myself that at last it was happening... *at last* I was going to give myself totally to the man I had loved for so many years. I had fantasized it, and yet somehow right now it was progressing too quickly. He was hot and eager for release, and I was slow to being fully aroused. Maybe it was the tranquilizers I had taken earlier that suddenly seemed to deaden the sensations I had been expecting to feel.

"Let's go to the bedroom," I suggested.

"Why?" asked Rob. "I want you here... now." The urgency in his voice told me that he was in command.

Part of me wanted him to be and took pleasure in his

dominance as he fell onto me again and kissed my face and groped my breasts. But then there was a part of me that wanted to rebel, a part of me all too familiar from my years as Alan's wife. I told myself it wasn't going to be like that and forced myself to respond to his needs. His breath was hot on my neck as he proceeded. I wanted him to slow down, to wait for me to catch up.

At the same time, I didn't want to disappoint him, so I let him go at his pace. As hard as I tried to enjoy it, I was feeling only the mildest form of pleasure from him. My mind was in turmoil. This was supposed to be the most beautiful, most fulfilling experience of my life—making love for the first time to the man of my dreams—and yet I was uncomfortable. He held me down so that soon all I could think about was catching my breath. And then, quite suddenly, it was finished. Rob collapsed on top of me, his warm skin moist and salty.

We lay there for what seemed a long time. Finally, I began squirming and Rob lifted himself. He looked at me questioningly for a moment, then a satisfied smile spread over his face and he leaned down to kiss me once again. "That was wonderful," he said. "How was it for you?" His finger wiped a stray hair off my forehead.

I forced a smile, then pushed against his chest. He took the hint and got up. I let out a sigh as we both sat up. I didn't want to lie. "How do you think?" was my response.

Rob grabbed me and hugged me. "You're beautiful." He reached for his clothes, then stood up. "I haven't been home yet, and I have some business to attend to regarding our doctor from Grand Rapids."

I stared at him in surprise. "Have you found out anything more about Dr. Gamble?" I asked hopefully.

"Not yet, but I intend to. I'm driving back up there tonight. If you want, you can come along."

I decided not to go. I told him I was expecting JoAnn and her friend to stop by later.

"Very well," said Rob when he was ready to leave. He

drew me toward him and kissed me. "Take it easy. I'll call you tomorrow. Or better yet, why don't we plan for lunch?"

I lingered in his embrace for another kiss, and then we made plans to meet at my office tomorrow at noon.

29

Rose's Nightmare

THAT EVENING JoAnn brought Dr. Spence to my house. I had been expecting a man in his late thirties, but was surprised to greet a man with white hair and glasses, who looked older than my father. I extended my arm and welcomed him with a puzzled smile.

Dr. Spence shook my hand. "Well, it's a pleasure to finally meet you, Winnie." He had a wrinkled but gentle face and blue eyes that came alive with his smile.

JoAnn leaned on his arm, her face aglow with my astonishment. She had expected me to be startled, and I was.

"Doesn't Winnie have a cozy house?"

"Oh, indeed." The doctor grinned as if it were only a dollhouse and we were all on *Captain Kangaroo*.

"Please sit down." I recovered from my bewilderment the best I could.

"Winnie, where's Rob tonight?" asked JoAnn.

I explained how he had taken a drive up north.

"Aw, it's a shame he couldn't be here."

"Can I get you anything to drink?" I asked.

"Sure." JoAnn grinned. "Martin, what would you like?"

"Well, if you've got any prune juice..."

JoAnn caught my expression and burst out laughing. "Isn't he a riot?"

Dr. Spence cleared his throat. "Whatever you have is fine."

I started into the kitchen and JoAnn stood up. "I'll come and help you." When we were alone, she asked, "Well, what do you think? Isn't he a dear?"

"He's married?" I whispered.

"Shh, he doesn't like to be reminded, you know. Oh, I know, he's so much older than I am—but don't you think he's kind of cute for an older man?"

I merely smiled. I didn't dare reveal my true feelings. We carried the drinks out and sat around and conversed awhile. I soon discovered that Dr. Spence was both intelligent and witty and had an office downtown. Although I didn't understand JoAnn's attraction to him, he was very friendly and easy to talk with. And it was obvious that he liked JoAnn.

"Winnie, why are you being so quiet tonight?" JoAnn asked.

"Am I? Maybe it's those tranquilizers you gave me."

Dr. Spence jerked his head. "JoAnn Gremel, did I hear correctly?" He eyed me disapprovingly. "*Whose* tranquilizers?"

I opened my mouth, but only stuttered.

"I thought they might help calm her down," JoAnn explained.

Dr. Spence wagged a finger at her. "Young lady, it is never wise to pass drugs onto others." He turned to me. "Taking medicine without a prescription can be very unwise."

"Well, after her experience at the Peltons', she needed something to relax her," said JoAnn.

"Yes, JoAnn told me about what happened over there." Dr. Spence sat back in the sofa and rubbed his chin. "I had a patient from that family a while ago. As a matter of fact, I was a good friend to Otto Pelton before he died."

"I didn't know that," remarked JoAnn.

"Otto was always a sensible man, had a good head on his shoulders."

"He was very amiable," I added, remembering the first and only time I had met Otto Pelton at the manor during my summer ten years ago.

Dr. Spence smiled. "In fact, I saw him for therapeutic reasons after he suffered his stroke."

I sat up straighter, suddenly interested. "Is that right?"

"Yes. I met with him at Spider Lake."

"And was he of sound mind then?"

"Well, as you may already know, Otto was unable to speak after he suffered his stroke. He was left paralyzed completely at first, but it is of my personal opinion that he lost none of his mental faculties."

"You said *at first*. Do you mean that as he started improving, he lost some of his paralysis?"

"He gained some control of his left arm, and I'm not sure about this, but I do believe he started to regain control of his speech centers again. Of course, nobody could understand anything he said after the stroke."

"Let me ask you something," I said. "Were you surprised that Otto Pelton died?"

Dr. Spence drew in a deep breath and let it out slowly. "Frankly, no."

"But wait a minute," interrupted JoAnn. "I thought you just said he was improving."

"Someone who has suffered a stroke is likely to have another," said Dr. Spence. "In Otto's case, even though he may have been recovering, I am not at all surprised he died."

I was lost in my thoughts and the conversation turned away from the Peltons, but I continued to contemplate what Dr. Spence had said about Rob's father.

Soon after, they decided to leave. I thanked them for coming by, then watched as they left, still unable to get over the fact that JoAnn was dating that man.

I had been unable to stop thinking about Rob ever since he had left that afternoon. My mind went over and over our session on the couch. I was angry at myself because the medication JoAnn had given me had affected me in some way that had prevented me from enjoying the intimacy. I had been unable to respond the way I wanted to, and as a result I now felt nervous and uptight. I was eager for our next time because then, I was quite sure, it would be so different... and satisfying for me as well as him.

I was preparing to go to bed early when the doorbell rang. I slipped on my robe, hoping it was Rob back from Grand Rapids already. I opened the door and Rose Pelton stood there, shivering.

"Rose, come in!"

"Thank goodness you're home," she said.

"Are you all right?"

"I'm freezing. It's really cold out there." Rose glanced out the door before I shut it. "I don't want to alarm you, but as I drove up, I thought I saw somebody in your bushes."

"What?" I peeked out the window at the row of shrubbery that separated my house from my neighbor's. I turned on the porch light, but it was still too dark to see much.

"It could have been my imagination," said Rose when she realized how concerned I was.

Deciding not to burden Rose with my suspicions about the ruddy-faced man with a beard, I said nothing. I hadn't been bothered with any more telephone calls or tailings since last week. I told Rose to sit down, then offered to make some hot chocolate.

"Thanks, Winnie."

"Rose, I'm so glad to see you. Rob and I were hoping you'd get in touch with one of us. We were worried about you."

Rose followed me into the kitchen, where I started heating the milk. "I heard about that poor housekeeper on the news," Rose explained. "I decided I'd better come home." We sat at the kitchen table. "My mother's just sick about it. We all are."

Being reminded of the disaster sent waves of aversion throughout me. The memory of Mrs. Hesselgesser's gray, prune-like face with the bulging eyes staring up at me filled me with dread. I felt I would never get the gruesome picture out of my mind. "Her family was contacted, weren't they?" I asked.

"Yes. And *you!* Being right with her when she died. Oh

Winnie, how horrible!"

I shuddered and tried to cast the image aside. "It's over now. Tell me, Rose, where have you been staying?"

"With a friend. I couldn't stay at the manor. That's why I came here. Mother asked me to stay, but I didn't want to." Her brown eyes, so much like Rob's, peered at me in desperation. "Do you think I could spend the night with you? I could just spread out on your couch and you won't even know I'm here."

"Rose, of course," I said. "I've got another bedroom. I'd love to have you. Stay as long as you like."

"I don't expect to stay longer than tomorrow," she said quickly.

I fixed our drinks and noticed while we talked that Rose kept trying to hide yawns. Because she looked so tired, I got out the sheets and blankets and made up the bed for Rose in the guest room.

"Thanks again, Winnie." Rose sank down onto the bed.

"If you need anything else, just yell," I said.

"Good night," she murmured.

I turned out the hall light and then returned to my room and read until my eyes wouldn't stay open. I fell asleep with the book on my chest and the reading lamp on.

Then, suddenly, I was wide awake. A shrill scream had rung out from across the hall. I bolted from my bed. Rose screamed again.

Without bothering to find my robe, I fled out of my room and flicked on the light to the guest room. Rose sat in her bed, sobbing. The covers were pulled up over her face.

"Rose!" I ran to her side. "What's wrong?"

Rose let the blanket slide away. "It was horrible," she cried. Her face was wet from tears.

"What? Did you have a nightmare?"

"Yes." She sobbed some more, and I sat down on her bed. "Oh Winnie, I thought if I came here, I wouldn't have the dreams like I do in the manor."

I put my arm around Rose to comfort her. "Was it about

Benjamin again?"

Rose shook her head and sniffed. "No, it was worse." She dabbed at her eyes.

"Well, let's not talk about it." I didn't want her to get worked up again.

"No, I *want* to talk about it. I need to. Then... then I think I can handle it, if I can just tell someone about it."

"Okay, if you think it will help."

"It was so horrible, Winnie. Instead of Benjamin's voice calling me, I heard my father." She buried her face and sobbed a little.

"You miss him a lot, don't you?" I said gently.

Rose nodded, then composed herself. "Then... then I was in this very small room, and it was dark and cold... and there were rats and spiders." She hugged herself. "And then there was this coffin. It was like a horror scene out of *Dracula*." She looked at me and her lip trembled. "Then the lid started to open, and it was creaking... and then all of a sudden, there he was! There was my father in this coffin with the cobwebs over him and the spiders... and Winnie, he sat right up and reached out for me!"

Rose buried her head in her arms again and sobbed.

30

Blowup

BECAUSE OF the dream, Rose and I couldn't get back to sleep. We sat up and talked for over an hour. I told Rose what Rob and I had found out on our trip to Spider Lake—about Dr. Gamble's odd behavior when her father's name had been mentioned.

"Something strange must have happened," admitted Rose.

"I wonder if Rob found out anything more," I said.

"I hope so," Rose said. "That's such a long drive to come home empty-handed."

When my alarm went off in the morning, I dragged myself out of bed and got ready for work. I didn't want to disturb Rose, so before I left, I wrote a note and insisted she stay another night if she wished.

At work I was behind in my duties, as expected, and spent the morning trying to catch up. Five minutes before twelve, Rob came by the office and I left on my lunch hour.

"Rose is at my place," I told him. "She spent the night." While we walked to the café, I explained about Rose's nightmare. "So I didn't get much sleep last night. What about you? Did you learn something more from Dr. Gamble?"

"Actually, no." Rob sighed. I suddenly realized he looked beat. I noticed a small nick on his cheek where he had cut himself shaving. His auburn hair was rumpled and unwashed.

He turned to me. "I'm glad Rose came back. I hope she'll go home. I feel my mother needs her right now."

"Your mother's still pretty upset about what happened yesterday, I take it."

"She's not at all herself. I think she's afraid to hire any more housekeepers. What's worse—I'm afraid none would care to work at the manor after what happened."

We arrived at the café and found a table in a secluded corner. The place hadn't been bombarded yet in the noon rush. We were able to order right away.

"Now tell me what happened with your trip," I urged. "Wasn't Dr. Gamble at home?"

"No. I tried to reach him through his answering service, but I was told he had left town."

"You mean on business?"

"Well, that's what I was led to believe... at first. But after I did some digging, I found out that he left for good."

"Just like that?"

"They told me he simply abandoned all his patients and nobody knew whether he was coming back or not. I'm afraid I couldn't find out anything more about him. But I did discover something even more peculiar."

The waitress brought our salads and drinks. After she left, Rob lifted his water glass to his lips and took a drink. "This morning," he continued, "I drove into town and saw Mr. Stiffler of Stiffler Mortuary. He's the one who took care of Benjamin's and my father's funerals."

"And?"

"He remembered my brother's funeral because it was such a tragic death. And he remembered my father's because of the way my mother reacted."

I waited for him to continue. He drank more water, then set his glass down.

"He said she was frantic. He also said that when he had talked to her, she had insisted he burn his spectacles and clothes—that she wouldn't have it any other way."

"How odd," I remarked.

Rob shook his head. "You know... my father never wore glasses in his life."

"Are you sure?"

"I'm positive. Ask Rose."

"*Fred!*" a voice rang out.

I froze with the water glass halfway to my lips. George approached the table. He had on a large bright sweater with the high school letters on it. He grinned at me in his usual jolly way. "I knew I'd find you around here somewhere," he said. "I stopped at the office, but they said you had already left." His gaze rested on Rob, and suddenly the eager grin melted from George's face. "Oh, I'm sorry. Am I interrupting an interview?"

"George Wyatt, I'd like you to meet Rob Pelton." I smiled to cover up my feelings of turmoil.

Rob reached out his arm, and they shook hands, but a baffled look remained on George's face.

"Do you work for the newspaper?" Rob asked George.

"What?"

"Do you work with Winnie?"

"No, Winnie and I are..." George caught the warning look in my eye, then cleared his throat. "Actually, Fred and I are just... friends."

Rob shot me a questioning look, then said, "Why don't you pull up a chair and join us? We just ordered."

For a worried moment, I thought George would accept, but he said, "Thanks, but no." He turned to me. "The reason I wanted to see you was to find out what time you want me to pick you up on Thursday evening."

I was puzzled. "Thursday?"

"Don't tell me you forgot." George chuckled. "It's bird night."

Then I remembered that Thursday night was the monthly meeting of the local Audubon Society, and George and I were in the habit of going together.

"*Bird* night?" Rob looked from George to me.

"Is the usual time okay?" asked George.

164

I could feel my cheeks growing hot. "I forgot about the meeting, George. I don't think I'll go."

"Well, okay. If that's the way you feel..." George shrugged. For the first time I could see a hurt look in his eyes. It made me want to crawl right under the table. "Fred, I just thought... well, never mind. I've got to get going. Nice to meet ya, Rob." He left before any more could be said.

I lifted the water glass to my lips and was embarrassed to find my fingers shaking. My cheeks were still warm.

Rob sighed deeply and spread out his napkin as the waitress arrived with the rest of our meal. After she left, he sighed again. "Don't you think that's kind of stupid?" he mumbled.

"What?" I asked.

"What he called you."

I picked up my fork. "What do you mean?"

"The name Fred."

"So? My brothers called me that all the time when I was growing up. It's short for Winifred."

"Well, it doesn't suit you. Who *is* that guy, anyway?"

I swallowed. "George is a friend of JoAnn's."

"It sounded more like he's a friend of *yours*."

"Well, yes, I guess he is." I took a bite of salad and tried to think of something to change the subject.

"Maybe you should let him know you prefer to be called Winnie from now on."

I looked over at Rob, who was staring at me curiously. He wasn't eating his food. "What do you mean?" I asked. I felt like telling Rob that I didn't mind what George called me. As a matter of fact, I liked it when he called me Fred. I certainly didn't see why Rob was getting so uptight about a silly nickname.

"I'm sorry. It doesn't matter." Rob smiled at me then, as if it really didn't matter to him. We ate the rest of our meal without further comment.

While we walked back to my office building, Rob remarked, "You know, it's funny about Marcia."

"What is?"

"She mentioned something to me about the other day."

I knew what he was referring to. "You mean, seeing me in the restaurant with George?"

"Now how did you know I was going to say that?"

I felt myself growing annoyed and I hated myself for it. "Well, so what if I had lunch with him? Can't I eat out with a friend?"

"It's not that," insisted Rob. He clutched my arm and drew me closer to him. "I'll tell you what I think it is. I think Marcia's jealous of you and wants to get back at you by telling me things about you. I know what she said can't be true. But then to see *him* walk in like that..."

"Rob! What things? What things did she tell you?"

"I can't help it, Winnie. I don't know what to think anymore."

I couldn't believe this was happening. My blood was boiling as I imagined what terrible things Marcia had conjured up about George and me after seeing us together in the restaurant. "How can you believe anything Marcia would say?"

He didn't answer me right away. "Well, why didn't you tell me about him before?" he finally asked.

I didn't know how to answer this. I turned toward the door to my building.

"It's because he means something to you, doesn't he?"

My lower lip trembled. "You're wrong. I've always been in love with *you—only you!* Maybe I just didn't think he was important enough to mention."

"Don't give me that!" His voice was hard. "I'm not a fool. I know better than that!"

"No, you don't!" I fled toward the elevator.

"Winnie!" he called after me, but I had reached the elevator and squeezed through the doors just before they closed. I sniffed all the way up to my floor, trying to hold it all in so that I wouldn't look like a fool in front of the newspaper staff.

31

Everything Turns Sour

ROSE WASN'T there when I got home that afternoon. I was disappointed she had gone, but felt relieved to be alone in my miserable state. I had been on the verge of tears all afternoon and now that I was home, I only felt more depressed.

When the telephone rang, I eagerly answered it, hoping it would be Rob. But it was George. He was the last person I expected to call after the way I must have hurt him in the restaurant. He sounded rather despondent.

"I thought you should know," he told me. "Your name's up for nomination Thursday night. They want you to be president next year. I thought you might reconsider going to the Audubon meeting."

This was news to me. I had been an active member of the local chapter for years. I had always supposed it was inevitable that some day it would be my turn to assume the executive role. For the moment I didn't know what to say.

George seemed to sense my surprise. "You should probably be there," he said. "If you like, I'll not go."

He was more depressed than I had thought. "That's all right, George." I didn't know what to say to him. My own heart felt heavy, and it just didn't seem fair to let George think there could be anything between the two of us. I suddenly wished I had been honest enough to tell him about Rob Pelton from the start.

"I guess this means you don't want to see me anymore," George said.

"Oh George, no! Don't think that way..." I trailed off because I knew it was better left unsaid. After the gap in conversation grew too long, I made up an excuse that my bath water was running and hung up. I felt lousy about George, but what could I do? I cared for him too much to have to hurt him any more than I had.

I waited around a little longer, hoping Rob would call, but when he didn't, I decided a long hot bath was actually a good idea. I soaked in the tub for half an hour, which helped a little, but the evening was a slow and lonely one. I ended up going to bed early, being tired from staying up the night before.

In the morning I felt refreshed, but still depressed. There was a trace of snow on the ground. I noticed the sun coming out and speculated that by noon all the snow would be melted away. If only my blues could melt away that easily.

I purposely stalled with my work so that I had to turn JoAnn down when she came in to see if I wanted to have lunch. I didn't feel like talking to her today, although it was probably what I needed most. In the back of my mind, I was hoping that if I waited long enough, Rob might come by, but he didn't. Finally, I went to lunch by myself.

"Someone called for you," Marion announced when I returned. "I took the message. It's there on your desk."

"Thanks, Marion." I found the note, which simply read: *Stop by Pelton Manor today. Urgent.* I wondered if Rob had called. When I questioned Marion, I was told the person who had called had been a woman. I tried telephoning the manor, but received a busy signal twice.

As soon as I was done with my work, I drove over to the manor. I couldn't help but have mixed feelings. For one thing, I wasn't sure if I was ready to face Rob after yesterday's little disagreement. I knew there was a chance he might not be there, and I was curious about the message. Had Rose been the one who had left it?

I drove up the driveway and parked my car beside Rob's. Rose's car was gone.

Marcia answered the door when I rang. "I'm glad you could come," she said without smiling.

I was surprised as Marcia led me into the living room.

"It's Irene," continued Marcia, "she's gone berserk."

"How do you mean?"

"I thought she'd be over it by now, but she's been this way since Mrs. Hesselgesser... you know."

"Where is she?" I looked around.

"Upstairs. I thought it would help if you could talk to her. She seems to take to you." There was mockery in Marcia's voice. She took a seat and beckoned for me to do the same.

"Is Rose home?" I asked.

"No. She came by this morning, but then she left again."

"Then she didn't call me?"

"No, *I* did." Marcia picked up a pack of her cigarettes and withdrew a stick. "You see, I wanted to have a few words with you, to set you straight." She had trouble getting the lighter to burn, and I noticed her fingers trembling.

"Is Rob home?" I asked, remembering his car parked outside.

"He left a little while ago. But no matter. What I have to say is only between you and me."

I felt a chill in the air and noticed my arms were covered with goose bumps. I didn't know what Marcia meant, and the hardened look in Marcia's eye scared me. "What is it, Marcia?"

"I know your kind," she scoffed. "You newspaper people are all alike—nosy and pushy. You came here with the intention of uncovering some dirt, didn't you?"

"No, Marcia. I'm not that way. Really, I'm not a reporter. And I resent your accusations."

"But you'll admit you're dying to get to the bottom of this tragic story. You want to know the god-awful truth, don't you? Don't you?"

I tried to act calm and crossed my legs. "Sure, I'll admit

that. Now suppose you just tell me what it is you called me over here for."

Marcia finally lit her cigarette and drew in, then blew out smoke. "You really want to know what happened that night my husband died, don't you? Well, first you have to know about Rob and Ben."

"What about them?"

"Their rivalry, or didn't you know?" There was no emotion in her voice now. "Rob resented Benjamin for marrying me." Marcia's eyes stared into blank space. "It was Rob who caused Ben to fall down those stairs," she said, "out of love for *me!*" Her eyes filled with tears, but her voice remained steady. "Your high school sweetheart is not as *innocent* as he seems, Mrs. Grant."

I was stunned. How could I believe a word of what Marcia was telling me? It wasn't true. Rob never loved *her*. He couldn't have. She was just trying to humiliate me into leaving Pelton Manor and never coming back.

"I know what you're probably thinking," Marcia told me. "But you've got to believe me."

I gripped the arms of my chair and challenged her. "Marcia, how could Rob be responsible for Benjamin's death? He was in Connecticut when it happened."

Marcia shook her head. She tried to blink the tears away, but they flooded her eyes. "No. He was here that night. Rob was at the manor the night Benjamin died."

"But..."

"You don't know him, Winnie. He was *here*." The cigarette in her hand trembled.

"Well, why didn't Irene..."

"She is protecting him," Marcia insisted. "She had lost one son already and she wasn't about to lose the only one she had left."

Irene appeared at the doorway to the living room then and we turned to watch her. It was as Marcia had said—she had gone berserk. Irene was dressed in a housecoat and her hair looked as though she hadn't brushed it in days. Her face was pale. There was a sunken look about her shallow cheeks. Her eyes darted back and forth as she entered the room.

I jumped up and went over to her. "Mrs. Pelton..."

"Where's Marcia? Where is she?"

"I'm right here." Marcia wiped her eyes.

Irene seemed to recognize me then. "Oh, hello, dear. How nice of you to come by. What's the matter with you, are you cold?"

"No, I'm all right."

"Well, I'm not. It's like an icebox in here. Marcia, turn up the thermostat."

"It's already at seventy-five," replied Marcia. "I just checked it ten minutes ago."

"Well, there's a draft coming from some place," Irene insisted. She patted my arm. "You wait here. I'll go see if Mrs. McCloskey is ready with the tea." She started into the hall.

I stared at Marcia, who called out to her mother-in-law, "No, wait, Irene. Let's not bother her right now. I don't want any tea. Do you, Winnie?" Marcia shot me a look of despair.

"Where is Rob?" asked Irene. "He should be here. Tell him Winnie is here."

Marcia helped Irene onto the sofa. "No, Irene. Rob left on an errand."

"Well, where did he go?"

"He didn't say."

"I must remember to tell Otto about the draft in this room," continued Irene. "I'm sure he knows someone we can call."

Marcia took me aside. "She's getting worse," she whispered. "She thinks Mrs. McCloskey still lives here—and worse yet, her husband! Winnie, do you think you can do something for her?"

I couldn't speak. There was a hard lump in my throat and I was still shaken from what Marcia had said before Irene had walked in. I shook my head and stared into the hallway. All I wanted to do was get away from there. "Mrs. Pelton..." I sat down next to the woman. "Is there anything I can get you? Do you want me to do anything for you?" I held her hand, which felt like ice.

Irene pulled away. "I want Marcia. Where's Marcia?"

"I'm here, Irene." Marcia turned to me. "Well, it was worth a try. Apparently you don't mean as much to her as I thought."

At that, I couldn't stand another second. I fled from the room, into the foyer and out the door. I was afraid to hop into my car and drive because of the way I felt, so I took off into the woods behind the manor. Maybe I could regain my senses so I could think clearly again.

I didn't know where I was going. I didn't care. I thought I should know better than to believe what Marcia had said, but somehow the tears in Marcia's eyes had convinced me that perhaps things were not as they seemed. I recalled the times Rob had tried to talk me out of thinking his brother's death had been anything more than an accident. For the first time, I wondered—had there been anything between him and Marcia? Had he really been at the manor the night Benjamin had died?

Remembering Irene's state of mind caused me to shudder. It was obvious she needed help. As I picked my way over dead leaves and branches, I made up my mind to call JoAnn when I got home and see if she could ask Dr. Spence to call on the manor.

I was about to turn back when I noticed I was close to the mill pond. I could see the top of the mill through the trees and it made me ache inside as I thought of Rob and the last time we had been there. Instead of turning back right away, I advanced toward the mill, drawn by the feeling of nostalgia it instilled in me.

I wandered up to the bank of the pond and stood, looking into the water and feeling comforted by the quiet gush of the waterfall that fed it. The pond was brown and murky, but I sat down on a rock and watched it for a few minutes. Not too far off, a train was coming. The chugging sound was getting nearer and its whistle echoed in the late afternoon air. The bare tops of trees stirred as a breeze pushed through them. I stared up at the tall abandoned building next to me and shivered. I wasn't dressed for the woods.

Now that I was more or less calm, I decided to head back to my car. Besides, it was growing dark.

Voices startled me. Two men were shouting. When I realized the noise was coming from the far side of the mill, I carefully approached the building. Then I saw that it was Rob with another man. Neither of them seemed to notice my presence, so engrossed were they in their argument.

The other man was large and wore a sheepskin coat. My chin dropped when I recognized the bearded man with the ruddy complexion who had stared at me in the bar and who had been snooping around my car. Not wanting to be seen, I drew back against a cottonwood tree and watched. I was too far away to make out any of the words, but it was obvious they were quarreling about something. What could it be? And why were they out here in the woods?

Then it clicked. I remembered where I had seen that man before. The morning I had gone birding—the same morning I had run across Rob at the mill—I had seen this man emerging from the woods by the cemetery. He had been carrying a rifle. He was the hunter in the black-and-red coat who had lifted his gun in my direction and then fled! Had he met Rob at the mill that morning? Was that the reason Rob had been in the woods? He had told me he had simply been out for a walk, but the coincidences suddenly seemed too great.

I stepped closer to try and make out what they were saying, but a twig snapped under my foot. Rob turned and saw me. The man in the sheepskin coat looked equally startled.

"Winnie!" Rob called out.

For a moment, I hesitated. I wanted desperately to confront him with my questions about the bearded man. I also needed to find out if Marcia's words had been true. But then I turned and ran. I stumbled, but got right up again and ran back toward the manor. I didn't know why, but I felt frightened.

173

When I could see the house through the trees, I slowed down. My chest ached and my breathing was staggered. My throat felt parched from the cold air, but I could only think of reaching my car and driving away.

As I passed the old estate, I gazed up and suddenly regretted ever coming there. I wished I had never met up with Rob again or gotten involved with any of the Peltons.

Then something peculiar caught my eye. I stopped and clung to a willow, still trying to regain my breath. Squinting because of the dimness of daylight, I searched the high windows of the manor, where I had seen something only a moment ago.

Then I froze. There it was again. In one of the smaller windows near the very top, a curtain swayed back and forth. Then I made out what looked like a human hand, clutching the curtain.

32

The Third Floor

I STOOD watching the high window until I saw the hand slide down against the glass and then vanish. I hadn't imagined it. Somebody—or some*thing*—was up there. I decided I wasn't going to leave until I found out what or who. Forgetting my personal woes, I ran around to the front of the manor and rang the doorbell.

Marcia was startled to find me. "Winnie, I thought you left."

I didn't wait to be asked in. "Where's Irene?" I asked as I pushed past Marcia.

"Oh, I don't know. She's around. Why did you come back?"

Looking up at the staircase, I decided I had to be calm about this whole thing. Somehow I had to get up to the third floor without anyone finding out. I invented an excuse. "I... I let Rose borrow a book of mine," I said, "and... and I need it back."

"But Rose isn't here," protested Marcia.

"I know, but I really need it. I'll just run up to her room and see if it's there."

Marcia frowned. "Well, okay ... but hurry up."

I sighed in relief. I had expected Marcia to react suspiciously, but she was simply annoyed. "I'll only be a minute." I started up the steps. Luckily, Marcia didn't follow me. I hoped Marcia would stay put long enough for me to slip up the forbidden stairway to the third floor without being discovered. I reached the hallway and hesitated a moment, then turned toward the dark flight of narrow steps.

Footsteps approached. "Oh, I didn't know you were still here, dear." Irene caught me by surprise. Still dressed in her housecoat, she had apparently emerged from one of the bedrooms. "Did you find Rob?"

I started to explain how I had come up to find the book, but Irene wasn't listening.

"I just know it's going to be lovely," Irene told me, clasping her hands with a dreamy smile on her pale, wrinkled face. "Why, we can hold the ceremony right here at the manor. Rose will be maid of honor."

I didn't know what she was talking about. Irene certainly wasn't in her right state of mind.

"I always wanted a wedding to be held in the manor," Irene continued. Her eyes measured me from head to toe. "And you, standing beside Rob—what a beautiful bride you'll make."

Irene didn't seem to notice me as I slipped past her and ran into Rose's room. There I waited until Irene was gone. Then, when I was sure no one was in the hall, I quietly made my way to the third floor stairway. I heard voices coming from downstairs. The door slammed, and then I heard Rob asking Marcia if she had seen me.

Unable to wait another second, I started up the narrow steps. I had trouble seeing in the dark and there was no light switch. A wave of guilt mixed with fear swept over me, but I climbed steadily. My heart seemed to pound between my ears and I felt scared of what could be waiting for me on the third floor.

Just as I placed my foot on the last step, something jumped out of the darkness at me. I screamed as a large heavy object brushed me—a body without a head. Every nerve in my being vibrated and I lost my balance. Suddenly, I was tumbling down the steps. I fell hard against the stairway wall and the rest was total blackness.

33

Rob's Denial

WHEN I regained consciousness, I was aware of a dim sea of faces. Rob held me. Then I recognized Marcia, Irene and Rose. As the numbness subsided, I became aware of a throbbing headache. I wondered if I was dreaming.

"She's going to be all right, isn't she?"

"Dear God, what happened?"

I made an attempt to get up, but Rob protested. "Don't try to move, darling."

"Why, she fell down these stairs," Irene said. "We heard her screaming and came at once."

"It seems she tripped on this old manikin," Marcia said. I noticed a sewing manikin lying on its side on the floor beside me. I started to focus a little better and began to speak. "Rob..."

"Are you hurt?" he asked.

I looked into his face and saw compassion. "I think I'm fine," I mumbled. "My head hurts."

"It's no wonder. You took a nasty fall." Rob held me and it didn't matter that everyone was watching. I just felt so secure in his arms. Now that I was fully awake, I began to feel a few bruises in my left hip and shoulder.

"What were you doing up there?" Marcia asked me.

Rose shot an angry glance at her sister-in-law and helped Rob slowly pull me to my feet. "Winnie, I'm glad you weren't injured."

"Rose, when did you get here?" My voice sounded groggy. I found out Rose had come home just as Rob had come out of the woods.

"Should I call a doctor?" asked Marcia.

"No, I'm fine," I said. "Really."

"Winnie, dear," Irene said to me in a stern voice, "you should not have tried to go up those stairs. I've told everyone for years what condition those steps are in. Now, I'm going to have to speak to Otto about boarding up that stairway."

I noticed Rose's look of alarm at the mention of her father's name. Rob led me through the hall, making sure I could walk by myself. We all went downstairs to the living room. Irene followed behind, scolding me the whole way.

I didn't tell anyone why I had climbed the stairway. But I remembered vividly the hand I had seen in the upstairs window. And somebody had pushed the manikin out in front of me at the top of the stairs to the third floor. I kept this to myself, as well, for I realized it had to be somebody in this house.

"You're staying here at the manor tonight," Rob told me. "I won't let you leave."

"He's right," Rose added. "You're in no condition to drive home. You can stay in the spare bedroom adjoining mine."

Irene was through scolding and seemed a little more coherent. She hugged herself and looked around the room. "My, but it's cold in here. Marcia, perhaps Mrs. McCloskey will build a fire for us in the fireplace."

"No, Mother," Rob said. "I'll do it."

"Well, then..." Irene sighed. "I will go see what she has planned for dinner."

Marcia left with Irene. Rose stayed with me as Rob went outside to bring in some firewood. Once he had the wood inside, Rose left the room, leaving the two of us alone. I was still shaken up from my fall and stayed on the couch, where I silently watched Rob as he stacked the wood in the fireplace and got a blazing fire going.

178

Then he came over and sat next to me and drew my head against his shoulder. "Why did you run away like that at the mill?" he asked me. His voice was soothing and I didn't move away from him, although the doubts I still felt from earlier continued to plague me.

Instead of answering his question, I asked, "Who was that man you were with at the mill?"

"I'm sorry if he frightened you," said Rob.

"Please tell me. I'm not ignorant, you know. I've seen that man more than once before, and you know it."

Rob caressed my cheek. "I'd be a fool to deny it." He sighed. "Okay, I'll tell you. His name is Lloyd Jarvis."

"How do you know him?"

"Actually, it's a long story. He had some business dealings with Benjamin."

"Why were you arguing?"

Rob sighed. "You mustn't concern yourself with any of this now. Believe me, it's not important. Right now the only thing that's important is you. Are you feeling better?"

"I don't know," I replied. The aspirin Rose had given me hadn't taken effect yet. It felt so good to lean against Rob's warm body and to stare across the room at the crackling fire which seemed to hypnotize me. I felt so drawn to him and was aroused by the wood smell on his clothes. Suddenly, I didn't want to think about the man in the sheepskin jacket anymore. Then I found myself asking, "Why didn't you tell me about Marcia?"

"What?" The question startled him.

I stared into the fire, unable to face him. "She told me about the night Benjamin died."

"What are you talking about?" Rob demanded.

The pain of Marcia's words that had never left suddenly mushroomed within me. My head pounded and I tried to keep from falling apart. "She confessed it was you who caused it," I said in a faltering voice. "You could have told me."

Rob grabbed my shoulders firmly. "Winnie, I don't know

179

what you mean. Obviously, Marcia has been feeding you a pack of lies. How could I have been here the night Ben died? She's out of her mind!"

"You don't have to pretend with me," I pleaded. "She was in tears when she told me how you were in love with her—how you and Benjamin were fighting because of *her*."

Rob stared at me in disbelief. "Winnie, get a hold of yourself. You're not rational. I never loved anyone but *you!*"

Something in his words eased the pain inside of me. Somehow I believed what he was saying, that Marcia had made it up. I gazed at his face, his brown eyes so full of compassion and love for me, and I wondered how I had ever doubted him.

34

A Ghostly Disturbance

ROSE AND Marcia had thrown together some leftovers and we sat down to a quiet supper. Irene did not eat. She had retreated to her room, and when Rose went up to tell her dinner was ready, Irene sent word down that she wasn't hungry.

"She hasn't eaten all day," Marcia said.

"What's wrong with her?" Rose was concerned about her mother and barely ate anything herself.

"She seems to have lost her mind," said Rob.

"I know, she believes Daddy's alive," said Rose, "and she keeps giving me orders for Mrs. McCloskey." Rose pushed her plate away from her. "Rob, we've got to do something."

"But what?" he asked.

I then suggested calling Dr. Spence, the psychologist, since I knew he had been associated with the Pelton family before.

"A shrink?" Marcia scoffed at the idea.

"Actually, I think that would be a good idea," said Rob. "We'll call him first thing in the morning."

After dinner I did the dishes. It was obvious that Marcia was avoiding me. I felt foolish for letting myself get taken in by Marcia's lies. I wanted to confront her, but gave up the idea as the evening wore on. What good would it do to gloat? Marcia was obviously a spiteful young woman who had lost her husband. I was convinced she had tried to drive me away from Pelton Manor—more than once, if my hunches were correct.

Later on, I joined Rob and we found a cozy corner in the library. The others kept to themselves in different parts of the house. This was the first time in a couple of days since Rob and I had spent some time together, just by ourselves. We snuggled together on the sofa and talked. We reminisced about the past and then began discussing our future.

"I'd like us to get married," Rob said as he fingered a lock of my hair, "and the sooner the better. I don't want to lose you to anyone else."

"What about your job?" I had to ask.

"We'll worry about that when the time comes," he said.

"You mean, I'll have to move to Connecticut with you?"

"Don't you want to?"

At one time I had thought I would go anywhere with him if he would only ask me. Now I stared down at my hands and began twisting the rings on my fingers. "It's just that Spundale is my home. When I married Alan, we moved away and I hated it. My friends are here now. I've got a good job..."

"But you won't need to work when you marry me," explained Rob. He took my hand and kissed it.

"Oh." I smiled. I had forgotten that my lifestyle would change. Suddenly I was saddened at the thought of never typing up another letter for Mr. Pendergast, or rushing people's last-minute ads over to Production after deadline. I would miss JoAnn if I moved to Connecticut with Rob, *and then there was George...*

"What's going through that pretty head of yours?" Rob tilted my chin and I looked at him. "Don't you want to marry me?"

"Of course. You know I love you."

Relief flooded his face. "That's all I needed to hear." He kissed me then, and for the moment I was overcome by my need to succumb to his hungry mouth and smothering embrace. It seemed like only a dream, yet here I was in his arms, promising to marry him—promising to marry the one man I had been pining over for ten years.

Our kisses grew deeper and more fervent until, at last, I had to beg for a reprieve. For a few moments I felt the thrill one must feel of achieving a lifetime goal. I would soon be Mrs. Robert Pelton. I lay contentedly in his arms as we lingered for a while longer. But I couldn't stop thinking of all the consequences ahead of me.

Rob sensed my reluctance and asked me again to share what was on my mind. I had been unable to get the memory of the hand out of my head, so I told him what I had seen in the high window of the manor that afternoon.

"Are you sure that is what you saw?" Rob sounded a little skeptical. But when he realized I was serious, a look of concern came over his face. "Still, you shouldn't have tried to go up there by yourself. Tomorrow I'm going up there to check it out. That is—if I can do it safely. Nobody's used those stairs in years. It's no wonder you fell."

Yet I reminded Rob about Mrs. McCloskey's tale about Irene coming down those stairs. I then explained to him about being pushed off my balance by the manikin. "That manikin didn't just fall out of place, Rob. Somebody was up there."

"You know what I think?" A smile curled the ends of his mouth. "I think being in this house has made you a little paranoid. Not too long ago, I remember you believing somebody had tried to drop a vase on your head. Well, never fear, my darling. The ghost does a lot of mischievous things in the manor, but he's never hurt anyone."

I forced a smiled, too tired to argue with him. When I went to bed, I took a book along from the library. Rose lent me one of her nightgowns. Although I was in the room right next to Rose's, I was apprehensive from the beginning about being there alone, if there really were such things as ghosts. It was easy to dismiss such ideas in broad daylight, but now that it was late at night and I was here between these old walls, fears that had seemed irrational to me before suddenly began to fester.

I couldn't get Mrs. McCloskey out of my mind as I fought

to concentrate on the novel before my face. I kept thinking of all the things Mrs. McCloskey had told me about ghosts and cold spots and seeing that man at the top of the staircase. I shivered under my blankets. It was freezing in this room and I just couldn't seem to stay warm. My toes were like ice as I drew my knees up to my chest. I struggled to hold the book open without exposing my hands to the cold air.

I had read a page and a half when something scraped against the ceiling. My blood seemed to stop flowing for a moment as I lay still, listening. After a minute, I went back to my reading, but another noise disturbed me. This time it was barely audible, but bumps and dragging noises seemed to come from above me. I could feel my heart banging inside my chest. I wondered if these were the scrapes and bumps Mrs. McCloskey had said she had heard.

Suddenly, I wanted Rob. I didn't care what anybody thought. I wanted to sleep with him in his room. I got up and threw on the robe Rose had let me use. Then I made my way into the hall. Just as I left my room, I met Rose coming out of her room. Rose's brown eyes were wide and fearful.

"Did you hear it?" she whispered.

"Yes."

"Come on." She beckoned me into her bedroom. We sat on Rose's bed and expected to hear more noises at any moment.

"What was it?" I asked.

Rose looked slowly around. Her eyes were moist. "I don't know."

"Are these noises that you've heard before?" I asked her.

"Well, yes and no. Oh Winnie, I don't think I can sleep."

"Me neither."

Another series of scraping noises and bumps followed just then. Rose and I huddled together and stared up at the ceiling.

"Rose, something's up there."

"Oh God," was all Rose said.

I quickly told her why I had attempted to reach the third floor that afternoon and Rose's face went as white as her pajamas.

"It's Benjamin." She trembled.

"No, Rose, get a hold of yourself," I chided.

"I know it's Ben," Rose whimpered, "like in the dreams. Oh God, Winnie, what are we going to do?"

"Whatever it is, I think we should find out."

"I didn't believe Mrs. Mac," cried Rose, "but now I do."

I sighed. "Well, we'll never know unless we go find out." I stood up.

Rose reached out and pulled me back. "Winnie, you're not serious. You're not going up there?"

"Well, no, but I'm sure Rob will if we tell him."

Together we left Rose's bedroom and started toward Rob's room. But the doorbell rang and the chimes resounded throughout the manor. We saw then that Rob's room was empty and dark with the door left open. Downstairs we heard voices, but they were muffled.

Rose and I started toward the stairs to see who had come to the manor this late in the evening.

"Yes, she's here," Rob's voice told someone. "But she's asleep."

We reached the balcony and looked down. I could make out the blond head of a man outside the door.

"Let me talk to her," he said. It was George.

"What could be so important at eleven-thirty at night?" Rob's voice had become hard. "Now get lost."

"I see no reason to get sore." George chuckled in his usual good-natured fashion. "I insist on seeing her."

"Well, you're not going to," said Rob. "She's in bed. You're going to have to wait till tomorrow."

"But I don't think what I have to say can wait until tomorrow. You see, by then I'll have lost my nerve."

"Been out for a few too many, I see." Rob's voice was still hard. "I suggest you go home and sleep it off, dude."

"I'm not drunk," George insisted. "I only want to see Fred." He tried to get past Rob, who immediately grabbed George's elbow with one arm and swung at him with the other.

Rose and I cried out when we heard the smack, and the next thing we knew, George had fallen back against the wall. I ran down the stairs, Rose behind me. My mind was in a turmoil. A storm raged within my breast.

"Rob!" I stood in the foyer and clutched my robe as the cold blast of wind blew in from the front door. I watched a crumpled George recover from the blow on the floor. I could only stare at him. His lip was bleeding.

"Why did you hit him?" Rose demanded, furious with her brother. The commotion had summoned Irene and Marcia from their bedrooms upstairs. Both of them stood on the balcony to see what was happening.

Rob turned to me. "I'm sorry, Winnie. I couldn't help myself." He reached for me.

"George!" I broke away from Rob's touch and knelt beside the man on the floor. "Oh George, are you all right?"

George glanced at me demurely and I could tell he had been drinking a little. He wiped the trickle of blood from his chin. I helped him to his feet.

Rob tried to make everything right. "Look, friend, I'm really sorry," he said to George.

Irene and Marcia climbed down the staircase and gathered around the rest of us in the foyer.

"Close that door, Rose," instructed Marcia, hugging herself.

"Look, I got carried away," pleaded Rob.

"Well, you didn't have to punch the man!" Rose shouted.

"Who *is* this?" Irene gestured toward George.

"I'm sorry if I woke everyone." George brushed off his pants and coat. "I just wanted to talk to Winnie." He stumbled over his foot but caught himself. Then he turned to me. There was such a desperate look in his blue eyes. "Aw, Fred... I can see I'm too late. It's no use, is it?"

I felt Rob put his arm around my waist. He drew me away toward the hallway. The storm still raged within me. I could barely stand to be there.

Irene began scolding no one in particular. Marcia and Rose had fallen into some kind of argument over what had happened.

"Well, I'll just be on my way," George slurred. He fondled his lip.

I felt miserable. This had happened because of me, after all. "Don't leave yet," I called out to George. I turned to Rob and said, "He's in no condition to drive home."

"Condition? What condition?" George slurred. "I'm not drunk, Fred."

Rob looked about to protest, but Rose went over and helped lead George into the parlor. "At least stay and have a cup of coffee," she said.

I could tell that Rob was annoyed with the whole idea. "What is this? The Pelton Drive shelter for derelicts and drunks?"

No one commented as we went into the parlor. Rose sat George down, then retreated to the kitchen to fix him some coffee.

Rob stood beside me while Irene began asking George questions that had nothing to do with the situation. "Winnie, I'm sorry," said Rob. "I didn't mean to hit him." He again reached for me.

Unable to tolerate another moment, I turned and walked back into the foyer. I started up the stairs when, suddenly, I noticed a sound. I then glanced up at the top of the staircase. What I saw dissolved all thoughts of Rob and George and the episode that had just occurred.

A human form was hunched over at the top of the staircase. Raising a frail arm, an old man who was very thin and pale stared down at me. His mouth was open and he struggled to speak, but couldn't utter a word. I could only stare in disbelief.

"Winnie, what's the matter?" Rose had just come out of the parlor with a mug of coffee. Then she looked up and saw the same thing. A piercing scream escaped from Rose. Then the coffee mug crashed to the floor and shattered to pieces.

35

A Shocking Discovery

WITHIN SECONDS, the others rushed in from the parlor. Rose and I still stood in the same spot, horrified at what we saw.

"Rosie! Winnie, what happened?" Rob followed our gaze. "What..."

Marcia gasped and drew back. "Oh my God!"

Rob swung past us and climbed the steps, two at a time. Rose spun around, and I saw that the girl was going to faint. Immediately I rushed to her side and caught her.

"It just *can't* be," Marcia moaned.

George helped me drag Rose over to a chair. She was starting to come out of it. "Who's that man at the top of the stairs?" George asked.

"This is impossible," cried Marcia.

"Dad!" Rob shouted at the top of the stairs.

I left Rose with George and followed Rob up the stairs, where a disheveled Otto Pelton struggled to raise himself. A sickly odor invaded the air as I drew near to him. Rob helped his father into a sitting position. The old man wore a pair of soiled pajamas, stained with sweat. He labored to catch his breath and seemed too exhausted to speak.

"Dad..." Rob's voice was choked from emotion. "What happened to you?"

"This can't be happening!" Rose called from below.

When Otto Pelton's eyes rested on his daughter, tears seeped from his eyes. "Rose..." His voice trembled and was barely audible.

"Daddy!" Rose tried to climb the stairs, but George held her back.

Rob turned to me. "Come on, let's get him down the steps. Will you help me?"

Without acknowledging, I helped Rob support Otto Pelton. Then we slowly ventured down the steps. The old man's skin was cold and moist, and he trembled violently. Finally, we reached the bottom and carried him into the living room and onto the couch.

I ran to the linen closet to get some blankets and a pillow. I was aware that George had found the telephone in the hallway and was calling for an ambulance. Irene, all of this time, stood and watched everything in silence. She seemed to be in a state of shock.

Rose turned to me. "Those noises... upstairs..."

I nodded. Without saying, we knew that Otto Pelton had been on the third floor. It was obvious he could not walk, but apparently he had managed to crawl and somehow work his way down the steps to the second floor. But how had he gotten up there in the first place? Otto Pelton was supposed to be dead!

The same questions were on everyone else's minds. Everybody talked at once. Rob tried to get some answers from his father, but Otto Pelton was simply too weary to speak. Within minutes we heard a siren as the ambulance arrived. The rescue crew wanted to transport Otto to the hospital, but the old man protested and raised such a fuss that the paramedics finally gave in.

"Let's at least get a doctor over here to look him over," said an EMT.

"Rose already called our family physician," explained Rob. "He's on his way."

"My father's been through a terrible ordeal," Rose added. "I think the worst thing we could do is move him. He wants to stay here with his family."

The telephone rang.

"Four months..." Otto uttered. He took a drink from a glass of water Rose had brought him. His voice was still strained.

"What are you saying, Dad?" asked Rob.

"Four... long... months."

"That's how long you were up there?"

Nobody had gone to answer the ringing telephone. I hurried into the hall to pick it up. It was Ophelia Pelton on the line. She and Aunt Pearl had been awakened by the sirens and flashing lights and wanted to know what was going on. I couldn't think of an easy way to break the news to them, so I simply said Otto had been discovered alive. Before I could go into detail, Ophelia hung up. I turned to call Rob and asked him if he would take his car over to get the aunts, but just then the telephone rang again.

"Hello," I said as soon as I picked it up.

"Put Rob on," ordered a man's voice.

"Who is this?" I demanded.

"Never mind. Just get him."

I informed Rob immediately and he left his father's side. Otto was resting and the paramedics checked his vitals again.

"Did your father say anything more?" I asked Rose.

"No."

George wandered in from the hall and announced, "The doctor is here now." His eyes met mine and I could tell he was sober again. I was about to tell him how glad I was that he was there when I felt a hand on my arm and spun around. Rob had on his coat. "I have to leave for a little while."

"Where are you going?" I remembered the phone call.

"Don't worry. I'll be right back."

"Rob, is anything wrong?"

"Right in here, doctor." George led the physician with his medical bag into the room. Rob brushed past them without answering my question.

"Otto?" The doctor stared in wonder at his patient who was

supposed to be dead. "Well, I always said you can't keep a good man down."

I ran into the foyer, but Rob had already gone out the door. I peeked out the window and saw him head on foot down the sloping lawn in the direction of the woods. Wherever he was going, it couldn't be far because he hadn't taken his car. I knew his sudden departure had something to do with that telephone call and my instincts told me the man who had called was Lloyd Jarvis.

"Fred?" George startled me and I jumped. "I'm sorry. I didn't mean to sneak up on you."

I held my hand to my heart.

"Are you going to be all right?" he asked.

"I'm okay." Another glance out into the dark convinced me that there was no time to lose. I turned toward the staircase and called to George as I ran upstairs, "I'll be fine." With all the commotion in the other room, I didn't think he heard me.

By the time I was dressed and back downstairs, the aunts had arrived. Pearl and Ophelia had walked over with flashlights from the cottage in the lane. I caught a glimpse of a teary reunion with their nephew as I slipped on my coat. Then I left the manor.

The cold and darkness enshrouded me as I hurried in the direction Rob had taken. The bitter cold air numbed my bare hands and face. Suddenly I felt foolish to be out past midnight. Chances were I wasn't going to find Rob. And even if I did, how was this going to look?

So much had transpired in the last hour, I couldn't begin to sort it all out in my head. Otto Pelton was alive! Apparently he had been living on the third floor of the manor for four months. How had he survived? All my stormy feelings about Rob had been shoved aside during the discovery of his father at the top of the stairs. Now they began to resurface as I recalled George's visit to the manor and Rob hitting him. A wave of frenzy surged within me.

As I approached the old abandoned mill, I noticed a truck

parked on the other side. As I drew closer, taking care not to make a sound, I saw the orange glow of a cigarette and heard men's voices. One of them was definitely Rob.

"Your time was up an hour ago," Rob's companion told him. I recognized the voice as that of Lloyd Jarvis.

"You can have the money," Rob pleaded. "And there's plenty where that came from."

"Boss don't give a rat's ass about your golden bucks, Pelton. He wants you back on the payroll."

"And I told you he can forget it."

"You really think it's that easy, don't you?" I watched as Jarvis threw his cigarette onto the ground.

"Just get out of here," Rob shouted. "Get the hell out of Spundale and leave me and my family alone!"

"You don't cooperate and it's going to cost you," Jarvis threatened.

"Go to hell!"

"It cost your brother plenty."

"Ben was a goddamned fool. He wouldn't listen to me."

"Well, maybe you should've considered that before you did him any favors."

Rob started to walk away. "I'm not going to listen to any more of this."

"I'm not done yet!" called out Jarvis. "And don't forget that pretty little widow you've taken up with."

I swallowed and tightened my coat. Could Jarvis be referring to me... or Marcia?

Suddenly, the headlights came on in the parked truck. Rob took off, but Lloyd Jarvis tackled him. As they wrestled on the ground, a figure inside the parked truck got out. I couldn't see him in the dark, but I was terrified for Rob. I knew they meant to possibly kill him.

Without thinking, I screamed. I called for Rob, then screamed again. The two men were on him now, and I knew there would be no mercy. I could hear his cries of agony and there was nothing I could do to help him.

Something brusque and heavy brushed me, causing me to stumble in the dark. Then I was aware of another person on the scene. I shrieked Rob's name several times before I realized that George was there and he was swinging his fists and dodging blows as though he had been in training. I watched in awe as George succeeded in knocking Jarvis to the ground. Then he started in on the other guy, who found an opportunity to escape back into his truck and drive away.

I immediately ran over and knelt beside Rob, who held his stomach and gasped. George was breathing heavily and nursing the back of his hand. "Rob," I cried, "you could have been killed!" I looked up at George. "Thank goodness you came!"

"I saw you ..." George panted, "leave the house... I was right... behind you."

"Rob?" I touched his shoulder.

George reached out an arm and helped Rob to his feet, but Rob broke away.

"Leave me alone," he growled.

"George just saved your life!" I protested.

"Winnie..." Rob wiped his mouth. "If you'll let me explain..."

"Okay, but let's go back to the manor," I insisted. My teeth chattered from the cold.

"You go on," George told me. "I'll stay here with him." He crouched beside Lloyd Jarvis, who moaned and groveled on the ground.

I told George we would call the police as soon as we got back to the manor.

"No need," he said. "Somebody already did. They should be here soon. Just send them over here."

Rob leaned against me and we started walking back to the manor. I could tell he was in pain from the beating. I had so many questions to ask, but decided to wait. I was shaking, both from the cold and the scare. Plus, I wasn't totally sure I wanted to know all the answers now.

36

Answers

WHEN ROB and I returned to the manor, a police car pulled up. We explained about the assault and battery and sent the officers over to the mill. Then we went inside.

The aunts were fussing over Otto, who was stretched out comfortably on the couch, sipping orange juice. His clothes had been changed and he seemed a lot more alert now. Dr. Sommers was talking to Rose and Marcia. I noticed Irene seated by the fireplace. The older woman stared with vacant eyes straight ahead.

"Rob, what happened to you?" Marcia gasped when she saw him.

"I'll be okay," he replied.

"Let Dr. Sommers take a look at that cut on your face," said Rose.

"Son," Otto called to Rob in a hoarse voice, "come here."

Rob went to his father.

"How is he?" I asked Rose in reference to her father.

"The doctor said he needs a lot of rest, but he's in good condition considering..." She sighed. "Oh Winnie, this is just too incredible. How can my father be alive?"

Rob cleared his throat. "Everyone, please! May I have your attention? My father wishes to speak. Will you all please sit down and listen?"

We took seats. In seconds, the room was still as everyone waited.

"It's true," began Otto. His voice was weak, but he managed. "I've been living in this house for the last four months."

The aunts gasped and looked at each other.

"But, Daddy..." Rose protested.

Otto held up his hand to silence her. "During the summer it wasn't bad. She brought me a fan and it was cool enough up there."

"*Who* brought you a fan?" demanded Rob.

Otto's eyes wandered toward Irene. "Your mother. But the last few weeks were so cold," he continued. "She said she'd bring me a space heater. I don't know. She must have... forgotten." The word caught in his throat. Otto took a deep breath and went on. "She took care of me. Good care... until last week."

"Mother..." said Rob as everyone began talking at once. Irene just stared into space and said nothing.

"But why?" cried Rose.

"Looks like the game is over, Irene," Marcia said to her mother-in-law.

"Do you mean to say you knew about this?" demanded Rob.

"You'd better start explaining." Rose glared at her sister-in-law.

"It all goes back to the night Benjamin died." Marcia's eyes fell on Rob. "But believe me, I didn't know what Irene was doing." She stood up. "I had no idea she was keeping your father up on the third floor."

"Well, go on!" Rose urged. I noticed that Rob's expression had changed from concern over his father to despair as Marcia spoke.

"Benjamin and I had a fight that night," Marcia explained as she knelt in front of the fireplace. "Irene was always siding with him. He had just come home that day from a business trip. Rob was home... and that's what caused it."

"What?" Rose stared at her brother. "I thought you were in Connecticut the night Benjamin died."

Rob shook his head. "No, little sister." His eyes slowly met mine.

"Rob and I were having an affair," confessed Marcia. With a hint of victory in her voice, she threw a glance at me. The aunts regarded each other knowingly and Otto slowly shook his head.

Rob stood up. "Marcia, no..."

"I *have* to," she protested. Turning to the rest of us, she tried her best to compose herself. "You see, Benjamin found out about it. Of course he was angry. He stayed out late that night. He came home drunk." She held her head as if it suddenly hurt. Tears began rolling down her cheeks. "He and Rob fought—*argued*, rather—and when I came out of the bedroom, Benjamin... he..." She sobbed and her words grew sloppy. "Ben... he... oh God... he'd *fallen*." She then broke down completely.

I stared across the room at the fireplace with its glowing embers dying out, one by one. Marcia had not been feeding me a pack of lies after all. Marcia and Rob *had* been lovers. Yet, the impact of her confession did not sting like it had earlier when I hadn't been sure it was the truth. Now I felt numb.

"*Rob*... it was *Rob* who pushed Benjamin down those stairs!" Marcia wailed louder.

"No!" stormed Rob. He stood up, defiant. "No, you're lying! It wasn't my fault."

"I don't believe any of this!" Rose jumped up and shook her head as if to deny all she had heard. "This is just some awful nightmare." She turned to her father and began to cry. "Daddy! How can you possibly *be* here?"

I went to Rose and tried to comfort her. Everyone had started talking at once.

"I will speak now," called out a calm voice.

The din subsided as everyone's attention focused on Irene. It was the first time she had spoken in an hour. She had emerged from her stupor and stood in the middle of the room. Her face was pale and I could tell she still wasn't herself.

"I didn't want Otto to say anything," Irene said. "At first he couldn't. He was in the hospital. Then he went to the resort. When he began to get better, I was afraid. I did the only thing I could."

"Let me explain." Otto struggled to sit higher. "Last July, Irene came early in the morning and said she was taking me home. I don't remember much of it because I was drugged. That renegade doctor gave me an injection..."

"Dr. Gamble?" I asked.

Otto nodded. "Yes, Gamble. That's the one."

"And Dr. Gamble signed the death certificate," said Rob. "For what, Mother? Two... three thousand?" There was an edge in his voice.

"I was afraid you and Winnie would find out something when you drove up to Spider Lake," said Irene. "But you have to understand, I did it for *him*—for Otto. I wanted him to get better at home."

"That explains why it was a closed casket ceremony," I said, "and why you had the mortician burn the clothes and the spectacles." I remembered Rob's investigation with Stiffler Mortuary.

"Then who was the corpse?" asked Rob. Out of the corner of my eye I watched the aunts wince.

"Some poor soul who had no family," replied Irene. "Dr. Gamble's patient from Grand Rapids. Dr. Gamble and I, you see, had the plan arranged for weeks. Finally his other patient died. He even helped me get Otto to Spundale, and we were careful to make sure no one was home that afternoon. It was easy. The dead man had no family."

"How could you?" Rose continued to sob. "Mother, how could you make everyone believe Daddy was dead?"

"Don't you see?" Marcia dabbed at her eyes with the sleeve of her bathrobe. "Irene was protecting your dear brother. She couldn't stand the thought of an unnecessary scandal. She knew your father would tell what happened when he recovered his speech."

"Just a minute." This time it was Otto who spoke up. "Tell about what? That I saw my eldest son, in a fit of anger, take a swing at Rob, and lose his balance at the top of the stairs?"

Marcia's eyes widened. "Ben swung at Rob?"

"That's right," said Rob, "but don't flatter yourself, lady. We weren't arguing over any mistake I made in the past over you." He sauntered over to the fireplace, where he sat on the hearth and nursed the cut on his face.

"Then what were you arguing about?" demanded Rose.

"The reason I came home in the first place," said Rob. "I thought I could help Ben. He'd gotten involved in some illegal investments. He was in way over his head. He'd asked me to help him before, and without even considering what might happen to me, I went along with it."

"Lloyd Jarvis was a business associate of your brother's?" I guessed.

Rob nodded his head. "Jarvis has been extorting me for months. Trying to get me back into the syndicate to replace Benjamin."

"Then that morning... when I was out in the woods and I saw you at the mill..."

Rob turned to me with pain in his eyes. "Jarvis met me there, yes."

I realized then that I had been followed by Jarvis on more than one occasion—that afternoon in the woods when I had left the aunts' cottage, and the time my car had been followed. It also explained the telephone call the day before Thanksgiving. I shuddered to think that I might have been injured or possibly killed in the syndicate's attempt to force Rob to cooperate with them.

"I've lived with the guilt of Benjamin's death for a long time," said Rob.

"But you didn't kill him," exclaimed Rose. "Daddy just said... he lost his balance."

"But if I hadn't been home that night... if Marcia and I hadn't..."

198

George came in from outside just then. He was dirty and disheveled. I got up and went over to greet him. I felt a wave of relief that he was all right. He told me the police had arrested Jarvis and had an A.P.B. out on the driver of the truck at the mill.

"She had rooms fixed up for me," Otto continued. "She brought my meals, even a radio, which she kept on low volume. But the last couple of weeks were bad. There's no heat up there and only a reading lamp. This last week she completely forgot about me."

"How did you manage to escape?" I asked. "And how did you possibly get down those narrow stairs?"

Otto started to tremble. Rose wrapped the blanket around him. "She would keep the door locked," he said. "I could move around a little. I used to keep myself from losing strength by crawling around on the floor."

"That would explain the scraping noises Mrs. McCloskey heard," I said.

"Then I discovered she left the door unlocked the last time she was up there to see me," said Otto. "I only wish I had found out sooner."

"It must have taken you hours to get out," said Aunt Pearl.

I told them, then, about the hand in the window. Otto explained that it had been his. He was able to peer out the window every once in a while and his greatest hope had been that someone might see him and come to his aid. I recalled that Greg Peterson, the paper boy, had most likely seen Otto at the window.

"I only wanted to take care of him," Irene whined. "I loved him. I never wanted him dead. I took good care of him."

"Keeping him a prisoner up in that attic room?" cried Rob. "Isn't that worse than death? His family not even knowing he exists?"

"Don't speak to her that way," Marcia scolded him. "After all, you're the cause of it all. She wanted to protect you!"

"What do you mean *he* is?" hissed Irene. She regarded

Marcia with an icy stare. "If it hadn't been for *you, * dear girl, intruding in our lives the day you stepped into this house with my eldest son! Why, I knew you would bring destruction and heartache, and not only was Benjamin too good for you—why, you had to weave your seductive web around Rob as well."

"How dare you talk to me like I'm some tramp?" yelled Marcia.

"If anyone's to blame, Mother, it's me." Rob paced back and forth. "What happened between Marcia and me was wrong, but it's been over since the night Benjamin died." His eyes fell on me, but I quickly shifted my gaze to the blankets I had gotten out of the linen closet for Otto.

"What happened to Mrs. Hesselgesser?" I asked. "Was it an accident when she fell down the stairs?"

"Of course it was an accident!" snapped Marcia.

"No," called out Irene, "it was no accident. I meant for Winnie to trip on that piece of rug. The foolish woman happened to fall instead. Winnie was onto something. I couldn't risk her finding out the truth."

"And the vase in the linen closet?" I added. "You put that there, too, didn't you?"

Irene scowled. "I didn't want you writing any articles on Benjamin's death."

"Mother!" Rose was alarmed.

"Then Winnie was right about the manikin," said Rob. "She didn't just trip over it."

"I had to stop her some way," replied Irene. "I panicked when she started up the stairs after me, because I knew she would discover me."

Outside, police sirens sounded. George walked to the window and said, "I told them to come back here."

Irene seemed to lose herself as she heard the sirens. As the aunts flocked around Otto and Rose, Irene turned to them. "Otto, dear, I only did what I thought was right. Tell them. Tell them how I fed you and cleaned you and brought you books when you asked for them. Tell them, Otto! Tell them!"

The old man's eyes closed tightly and he shook his head back and forth in pity. Irene started wailing in a morbid tone until the police came and took her away. The doctor left Otto in the care of the aunts and followed the police out.

Rob walked over to me and took my hands in his. "Winnie, I'm sorry you had to find out this way."

I felt the storm raging within me again. I wished more than anything at that moment that I could find it in my heart to forgive him. My heart ached so much in that moment, maybe because I had loved Rob Pelton for so many years. I had kept that love burning in the pit of my soul, without really knowing him. A love this deep, I realized, could not dissolve in an hour's time just because he had lied and deceived me. Yet, he had denied every word when I had confronted him earlier. I felt no mercy.

"You're the one I love," he said and his eyes probed deeply into mine.

"How can you stand there and lie," I challenged, "when we both know it's Marcia you want?"

"You're wrong," he insisted. "Whatever happened in the past is over now. I love only you. Please say you forgive me."

I couldn't say it.

"I'll make it up to you," he pleaded. "I promise. We've got the rest of our lives ahead of us. Let's move to Connecticut and put the past behind us once and for all."

I remembered something JoAnn had said to me once. "You can't relive the past." I withdrew my hands from Rob's. It would be so easy to surrender and say I forgave him and then fall into his arms. I needed to be held right then. I needed to be loved. I needed his strong arms to support me as I felt my world crumbling away.

But looking into his face, I no longer saw the man I thought I knew. Suddenly I didn't seem to know him at all. I turned and walked into the hall.

"Winnie, come back!" Rob called out.

I ran up the stairs to the bedroom and gathered my things.

As I was leaving, I met Rose in the upstairs hall. Rose looked exhausted and her cheeks were flushed from being out in the night air.

"Winnie, you're staying, aren't you?"

"No, Rose. It's for the best."

"But why? Oh Winnie, I really believe Rob loves you..."

I hung my head and said nothing.

Rose touched my shoulder. "Will you be all right?"

I tried to pull myself together. I would miss Rose more than anyone. She had become like a sister to me. The pain throbbed within me as I dared to look into her face. Then my eyes blurred. In that second Rose seemed to read my mind and realize the truth.

Then we fell into each other's arms and I choked back the sobs. Rose gently pulled away and smiled. "I understand, Winnie, and I wish you every happiness."

"You too, Rose." I wiped my nose. "You've got your father back. And I don't think you're going to have any more dreams about Benjamin." Then I asked, "Are you planning to stay now?"

Rose flickered a smile. "I think so. I mean, I *want* to. My dad is going to need me now." She stepped toward her bedroom, then turned around. "Oh. I think somebody's waiting for you outside."

I went downstairs. Rob was still standing in the same spot where I had left him.

"Don't go," he pleaded. "I love you."

The words churned within me. It was torture. I wondered at that moment if I would ever get over my feelings for Rob Pelton. He reached me just as I was going out the door. He seized me and turned me around. Then he kissed me, long and hard, hungrily clutching me to him.

I felt wetness on my nose and tasted salt. I didn't resist, but neither did I respond. It would have been too easy to give in.

"Goodbye, Rob." I broke away.

The flashing lights from one police car circled in the cold

night air. A few people milled about in the driveway, and I caught a glimpse of Ralph Pendergast and Mike, the staff photographer, from the *Spundale Star*. I could already see this week's front page headline: DECEASED OTTO PELTON DISCOVERED ALIVE.

Mr. Pendergast would undoubtedly get out an extra edition, since the paper had already gone to press. At least I still had a job to return to in the morning. I wasn't sure at that point about the rest of my life.

"Hi, Fred."

I swung around and met George. He smiled and stood beside me as we watched the police car drive away. Marcia stood in the cold with a coat thrown over her bathrobe. She began answering questions from the press.

"What will happen to Mrs. Pelton?" George asked.

"She'll be facing murder charges because of the housekeeper, Mrs. Hesselgesser," I replied, repeating what I had heard Rose discussing with the doctor earlier. "Even if they're dropped, she's going to need a lot of psychiatric care."

George grimaced. "For sure. Imagine keeping your husband a prisoner after faking his death."

"I know. She tried to harm me more than once, but she wasn't in her right mind." I shuddered from the cold.

We walked to our cars, parked next to Rob's and Rose's near the road. "What about Rob?" George asked me.

"I doubt if any charges will be brought against him." I said. "After all, Otto did clear him, and he was the witness when Benjamin died. As far as his involvement with Lloyd Jarvis goes..."

"That's not what I meant." George stopped and I turned to look at him. I couldn't see his face in the dark.

Suddenly, it dawned on me that George had come to the manor with a purpose. I looked back at the dimly lit manor. The willows shrouded it and the full moonlight cast a spell of gloom over the yard. "Tell me something," I said to George, "do you believe in ghosts?"

George laughed nervously. "No, do you?"

"I'm not sure," I said. "But I believe in something." I didn't tell George, but I believed Mrs. McCloskey really had seen Benjamin's spirit at the top of the stairs. As I recalled Rose's nightmares, I really believed Benjamin had tried to get through to Rose in her dreams—beckoning her to discover the truth.

"Let's take my car," said George. "We can come back for yours tomorrow."

I didn't protest. We walked, huddled together, toward his car.

37

Fulfillment

WE STOPPED at an all-night coffee shop and ordered some breakfast. The evening's events finally started to unwind from around us. I filled George in on what had been disclosed while he had remained at the mill, waiting for the police to arrive.

"You know, you never said why you came to the manor tonight," I reminded him.

"Oh... that." George shrugged.

"What was so important?" I asked.

George sighed, then drank from his mug. It was strange. George was his usual jovial self one minute, then a brick wall that I couldn't penetrate the next. Something was definitely bothering him, and he had apparently made up his mind not to let me in on it. After a few minutes of unbearable silence, I finally gathered up my purse and coat and told him I was ready to go home.

"Wait a minute, Fred." There was an urgency in George's voice that I had never heard before. His hand covered mine, as if to keep me from leaving. The penetrating warmth of his skin soothed me.

I looked up and saw that his blue eyes were looking into mine and that they appeared bluer than I had ever seen them. As hard as I tried, I couldn't seem to turn away from him. Some force grabbed hold and filled me with a realization I had been trying to smother.

"Rob was right," George said. "I went out and had a few too many tonight. I guess I was depressed. I realized after I saw you with him in the restaurant that you could never care for me—the way I cared for you—and still do, Fred."

I sat quietly and studied him.

"But I aimed to hear it directly from you," he continued. "I couldn't be satisfied until I heard the words. When you weren't at your house, I didn't know what to do, where to find you, so I got the address and drove over to the manor to see if they knew. Then to see your car was there and that you were spending the night..."

"Please take me home now..." I interrupted.

George tipped the coffee mug and drank the rest, then left a bill on the table as we got up to leave. The new feelings within me were not really new, but I was so overcome by them that I couldn't speak.

We rode to my house in silence. I glanced at George often as he stared straight ahead, intent on his driving. His messed-up hair and unshaved face struck me suddenly as appealing. There was a definite magnetism about him.

When we pulled into my driveway, we both hesitated. He usually would get out of the car first to open the door for me. Instead, he kept his hands on the steering column and slowly turned to face me.

"Only a few hours left till daylight." The softness of his voice carried me away.

"Suddenly I'm not very tired," I uttered. I couldn't take my eyes off of him. "George," I said, "why don't you shut off your motor?"

He didn't move, but gazed at me, unsure.

I slid toward him in the seat and snuggled against him. "And don't forget your headlights," I added. "You might run down your battery."

He automatically slipped an arm around me and pulled me

toward him. As his face leaned toward mine, he replied, "No chance of that." And then our mouths touched. At first he was like an innocent boy as we kissed. Our lips met several times, gently and briefly.

"George," I said, pulling away.

"What?" He blinked, on his guard.

"Let's go inside." I smiled.

He reached over and opened the car door. Taking my hand, he drew me outside into the moonlight. Then he held me and again we kissed. We went into the house, but we didn't turn on any lights.

I led George to my bedroom, where the moonlight spilled onto the bed. I didn't bother to close the blinds. Instead, I pulled George onto the bed and we held each other, bathed in the blue moon glow.

"Fred," he murmured, "are you sure this is what you want?"

I sighed. "Absolutely." He kissed me again, this time fervently, and I came alive in every zone of my being. At last I felt myself responding as a total woman. At last I knew what felt right.

He was perfect and I had been so blind. It thrilled me to no end that George, in his tenderness, could also be this passionate. As our kisses evolved, I welcomed his explorations and guided his loving hand to my breasts as I undid my blouse for him.

In my haste to leave the manor, I had stashed my bra in my purse. Now my soft orbs caught the moonlight through the window and George's finger gently caressed each one. The tingling it produced sent little shock waves through me and I lay my head against his strong shoulder.

He continued to fondle me, always returning to kiss my lips and invoke a new set of sensations that continued to spiral upwards. I gazed into his blue eyes and found myself held in the warm comfort of his tenderness. I knew now it had been George in my dreams. I had denied him, due to my obsession with Rob. But here was the one man who truly cared for me, a man who took his time with me, whose touch was so moving and was causing me to respond in a way I never knew possible.

"Fred," he whispered, "you are the only woman for me."

"Oh George..."

"Are you sure this is what you want?" he asked again.

I couldn't believe he had asked. "Yes," I breathed. "George... you're all I want. I know that now."

"I still want to make you my wife," he said.

"I will marry you," I told him with a smile.

For a moment he looked surprised. "You will?"

"Yes, George."

He looked at me with such love in his blue eyes. "I love you, Fred."

I fell onto him and we embraced and kissed, our mouths exploring each other as we rolled around on the mattress. The moonlight from the window created a sensuous blue glow that illuminated our feverish bodies. The next moments were filled with such passion and ecstasy, I was completely swept away. I didn't think about anything but the beautiful sensations George was creating with my body. My cries rang out as the feelings built, higher and higher.

At last we could hold back no longer. With a cry of desperation, I seemed to explode in a fiery eruption of frenzy. As the sparks flew out in all directions in my mind, my body quivered and quaked in its climax, and as the delicious sensations ebbed, I realized that this was the happiest I had ever been in my entire life.

For several moments afterwards, we lay pressed together, sweat mingling and heartbeats racing as our breathing slowed. I felt incredibly complete for the first time in my life. I realized George had made me forget... whoever it was I was supposed to forget...

38

Epilogue

WE LINGERED in each others' arms and watched out the window as the moon dodged in and out of the cloud cover. "Look, it's snowing," George told me.

Outside I could see snowflakes, thick and heavy. They swirled and plunged downward. Only an hour ago the moon had been shining brightly at Pelton Manor. Now it was losing itself in the approaching shower. There was no doubt about it. Winter had arrived.

"We could go outside," I suggested.

"And do what? Build a snowman?" He chuckled.

"A snowman and his snow lady," I teased.

"We could," he said. But we didn't. It was too comfortable lying there in each others' arms.

Snow was sticking to the ground a short time later, after George left to drive home. I looked out the window and waved as he backed down the driveway.

After washing up for bed, I pulled at the rings on my finger. To my surprise, they came right off. I studied them in amazement, then set them aside on the dresser as my eyes fell on something that had been left there.

It had been read and handled many times while my parents had been there and I hadn't put it away. I reached over and folded the scrap of newspaper. It was my news article on Pelton

Manor. I stood clutching it as events ran through my mind. It seemed so unreal somehow. I wondered if I would ever be the same.

Then I sighed and folded the article slowly and neatly. In the morning it would go into my jewelry box along with my rings—among other souvenirs of the past.

About the Author

Ann Carol Ulrich (Miller) was born in Madison, Wisconsin and grew up in the suburb of Monona, where she was known as Ann Schumacher. She loved writing fiction as a child and completed two novels before finishing high school.

After earning her degree in Creative Writing at Michigan State University, she moved with her husband, Jeff Ulrich, to Colorado and helped raise three sons. It was while living in East Lansing that she was inspired to write the first draft of this book, which was then called *The Ghost of Pelton Manor*, which is set in Michigan.

She has worked for various newspapers around the country and has many interests, which—besides writing and publishing—include music, art, nature, and raising chickens.

She loves living in the mountains, where she resides in western Colorado. Her favorite genre is romantic suspense, which includes *Sonata Summer* and *Rainbow Majesty*, the latter of which was a Finalist in the Eric Hoffer Book Awards. She also writes for young adults and has produced two memoirs, *Throughout All Time* and *Stepping Forth, An American Girl Coming of Age in the '60s*.

AnnUlrichMiller.com